To Lauren Ruth Rasula
With our Love
Christmas 1958.
Grandpa & Grandma
Hansen.

Laurie Rasula

Winter Cottage

Winter Cottage

by Carol Ryrie Brink
drawings by Fermin Rocker

THE MACMILLAN COMPANY, NEW YORK
COLLIER-MACMILLAN LIMITED, LONDON

WINTER COTTAGE
is for the boys and girls
who for many years
have had fun at our
SUMMER COTTAGE

CONTENTS

Winter Cottage

OCTOBER WOODS

THE VINCENTS' SUMMER COTTAGE IN NORTHERN WISCON-
sin had been empty for two months. From mid-August
to mid-October no one had banged the screen doors,
or run down the path to the lake, or put the canoe in
the water. It was a civilized cottage when the Vincents
were there, with their pretty clothes and automobiles
and vacation visitors, but when they were gone it became secret and furtive, like the little furry creatures
that prowled in the woods behind it. Its paths were lost
in leaves and its chimney whistled in the wind. The field
mice began to come in then, for they found it a very
agreeable place in which to winter, and the woodchuck
family took up their winter quarters under the floor of
the kitchen. The cottage might about as well have belonged to the woodchucks as to the Vincents, for the
woodchucks spent nine or ten months of the year there,

while the Vincents spent only two or three and sometimes none at all.

The cottage had once been a farmhouse built by an
early Scandinavian settler. It had double walls, low
ceilings, and plenty of stoves to withstand the intense
cold of a Wisconsin winter. Perhaps the farmer who
built it had thought too much of the fine lake view and
too little of the fertility of the land, for he had given
it up with scarcely an acre cleared. The Vincents had
added screened porches and a fireplace, but otherwise
they had changed it very little. Now, in the fall of 1930,
it stood dreamy and remote in long waving grass, listening to the sighing of the wind, and the rustle of falling
leaves.

Nineteen-thirty! That was the beginning of the great
depression, and for many people it would be a hard
winter. Banks had closed and many businesses had failed.
Honest people, who had lived comfortably all their lives,
suddenly found themselves selling apples in the street
because there were no jobs to be had. Even the dishonest people, who sometimes hid out in this lonely
country, were poorer than they had been. So little money
was available that everybody, good or bad, suffered.

At the close of a damp October day the silence of the
woods was broken by the sound of a car rattling and
chugging on the road behind the cottage. It was a lonely
road, and, even in summer, the city cars took the hill
quietly. But this car sounded like a hardware shop on a
holiday. It was small and very old, with a rickety trailer
swinging crazily along behind it.

With a cough, a gasp, and a sigh the old car reached

the top of the first hill and the engine stopped turning. Still rattling, but no longer coughing and sighing, it coasted down into the hollow at the back of the Vincents' place, and stopped dead still. The silence of the wet October woods settled around it.

The door of the car was flung open and a girl of about thirteen sprang out.

"Pop, you forgot to get gas!" she cried reproachfully. She broke a small branch from a near-by sumac and stuck it experimentally into the gas tank. "Nope," she added after a moment's silence. "We've still got some gas. I wonder what's the matter."

"She's boiling, Minty," said a smaller girl, sticking her head from under the flapping side curtain of the back seat.

"That's nothing," said Minty, "she always boils."

"Maybe she'll go up backward."

"I thought of that. If it's because the gas is low, we can probably make it up the next hill backward, but I don't know what we'll do with the trailer. What do you think, Pop?" The girl called Minty went up to the side of the car and addressed herself with determination to the thin, dreamy little man with the bristling mustache who sat in the driver's seat. "What do you think, Pop?"

"I was just thinking of the words of the poet Wordsworth," said Pop. "*It is a beauteous evening, calm and free—*"

"I know, Pop, but it's going to get cold later. We can't stay out here all night. I think we're on the wrong road."

"Listen," said Pop, holding up a warning finger. "It's that autumnal silence. You don't even hear a frog, now do you?" The two girls listened.

"Nope, no frogs. But think, Pop, what're we going to do?"

"Do? I'd like to stay right here, far from the city's madding crowd. *The world is too much with us, late and soon, getting and spending, we lay waste our powers—*"

"Look, Pop," cried Minty with exasperation, "the poet Wordsworth never tried to run a car like this. It's no use quoting him."

"You're right, as always, Minty," said Pop agreeably, "and I s'pose we've got to get along toward Aunt Amy's." He whirred the starter several times, but nothing happened.

"Why don't we leave the trailer?" asked the small girl, who, with a large and friendly dog, and a pile of luggage, was occupying the back seat. She appeared to be about ten years of age and answered to the name of Eggs.

"And leave all of our groceries?" cried Minty. "Goodness knows, they're all we've got left. We'd better hang on to the trailer." Pop got out and walked all around the car and looked. Presently he tried cranking it, but it seemed to have lost interest in life. He lifted the hood with a businesslike air and looked inside.

"Be careful, Pop," warned Minty. "You know the time you thought you were fixing the gas line and you made the short circuit."

"And the time you dropped a nut into the radiator fan," piped Eggs from the back seat.

"All right. All right," said Pop. "You girls think I'm no mechanic, don't you? Haven't I told you I was a plumber back in nineteen-ten?"

"Yes, but, Pop, you've been a carpenter and a printer and a groceryman and ever so many things. You can't expect to be good at all of them," said Minty sensibly.

"That's true," said Pop, "and I don't think I was a very good plumber. I stuck it out six months, and then the boss he said to me, 'Mr. Sparkes,' he said, 'I believe your talents lie in other fields.' I've always re-membered that. I thought he put it very elegantly. An educated man, the boss was." Pop shut down the hood again and climbed into the car. "Well, it looks as if we'd have to spend the night here tonight. Minty, you might as well get the quilts out of the trailer. It's likely going to be cold."

"Can we get out?" asked Eggs.

"I see no reason why you can't," said Pop, comfort-ably preparing to light his pipe. With shouts and barks of delight, Eggs and the dog, Buster, deserted the back seat for the misty wood.

"Don't get lost," called Minty, as she struggled with the damp canvas cover of the trailer. Minty felt cross. She didn't like being stuck here in these strange woods on a lonely road where no one was likely to come by with help. Yet she certainly didn't want to be back in Chicago where everything had been going wrong for them, and she didn't care to think about Aunt Amy's house which lay ahead of them. She was good and tired of being the only practical one in this family. Here was Pop perfectly happy to be stuck in a place like this as long as he had his pipe and a head full of poetry. Pop and Eggs could lay their heads down anywhere and never care a rap or know the difference, but Minty wasn't like that. She wanted to know where she was and why and for how long. It was difficult to be angry with Pop, because he was so easygoing and good-natured himself, but at this moment Minty very nearly was.

Suddenly there came a shout from Eggs.

"Say! There's a house here! It's not all woods. There's a house, and a kind of road all covered with leaves. Come and see, Minty."

This interested Pop. He knocked the ashes out of his pipe and got out of the car. "Maybe we can get a tow," he said.

Minty left her struggle with the wet ropes and ran along beside Pop. Just ahead of them Eggs and Buster scuffed and gamboled through the yellow leaves. Around a bend they saw the Vincents' cottage.

"Look! There it is!" shouted Eggs triumphantly. "Aren't I a good finder? There's a pump by the back door. Let's get a drink."

"You better wait and ask," called Minty. But Eggs had already started to work the pump handle up and down. It made a lonely screech as if it needed oil, but presently a stream of bright, clear water began to flow from the pump. Eggs put her mouth under the stream of water and drank.

"Um! Good!" she said as she came up gasping and wet.

"The house looks empty," said Pop. They peeped in a back window and saw a kitchen full of shadowy shapes. They could make out a stove and a gleam of pans on the wall and some provision tins on the shelves.

"If we could get in," said Eggs, "you could make us some pancakes, Pop."

"That's not a bad idea, Eglantine," said Pop. "I see they have a woodbox full of dry wood." Minty had moved on to the next window.

"They've gone away right enough," she said. "See, they have bunk beds and they've piled their mattresses all on the top one so the mice won't get at them. It looks as if they'd gone for a long time."

"A right cozy little house," said Pop with approval. "A family could be real comfortable here."

"Oh, look at the view!" cried Minty, coming around the front of the cottage in sight of the lake.

A shaft of sunlight had broken through the clouds and sent a long ripple of gold across the silver surface of the lake. Along the bank the silver birches with their thin covering of yellow leaves repeated the note of silver and gold, and on either hand the oaks still clung to their scarlet leaves. There was not another house in sight, not a boat, nor a human being stirring. Pop and Eggs and the dog came and stood beside Minty and gazed at the lake. They drew in deep breaths of the pure, frosty air.

"Um-m-m!" said Minty. "Doesn't it smell good? It sort of cleans you out inside." The sadness and anger

she had just felt began to lift away from her.

"It don't smell much like Chicago," observed Eggs. "No smoke or gas or stuff."

"Breathe in a lot," advised Minty. "I expect Minneapolis will smell pretty much like Chicago. Why didn't we ever live in a place like this, Pop?"

"Well, I don't know," said Pop. "We never did."

"I guess the poet Wordsworth would have liked this, eh, Pop?" asked Eggs.

"Yes," said Pop. "I think I may safely say that the poet Wordsworth would have thought this pretty nifty."

"I hear a stream, too," said Minty. "Look, Pop, it comes down over yonder and runs into the lake."

"I'll bet there are fish in that lake," observed Pop. "You never saw me catch a fish, did you, Minty?"

"No, I never did. I guess you'd be good at that, Pop."

"Yes, I am. It's just my kind of job—you know, sitting down—and lots of patience." Eggs began exploring again.

"Say, the screen porch is unlocked," she called, "and they've got their canoe up here in the porch. The front door is locked all right. But say! lookee here! This window that opens on the porch isn't locked. Come here and help! I think we can get in if we want to."

"Well, we'd better not," said Minty. "It isn't our house."

"We wouldn't hurt anything."

"But you can't just break into people's houses, Eggs. That's housebreaking."

"Maybe it is in Chicago. But I shouldn't think it would be way out here. We aren't going to steal anything."

"If they were at home," said Pop, "I guess they'd give us a night's lodging and not leave us stalled in the wilderness."

"Yes, but they *aren't* here," objected Minty.

"That's just the point, Minty," said Pop. "Since they're not here, they'd expect us to help ourselves. That's one of the first laws of the wilderness." Eggs and the dog were already crawling through the window, and Minty hated always to be a wet blanket to the enthusiasm of the others.

"I'll tell you what we'll do, Minty," said Pop. "We'll use everything real carefully, and, when we go, we'll leave some money on the table to pay for our night's lodging, just as if we'd stayed in a tourist camp."

"We haven't got much money to leave," Minty said. "You know there's just about enough to get us to Minneapolis."

"I know money's tight, but we have enough for one or two more tourist camps. We'll leave the money here instead."

Minty gave up.

"All right," she said. She followed the others in through the open window.

· 2 ·

PANCAKES

IT WAS ALMOST DARK INSIDE THE COTTAGE, BUT PRESently Eggs found a tin box full of matches and Minty found a kerosene lamp.

"Say, did you ever see anything like this before?" she shouted. "Pop, can you show us how to light it?"

"Hah!" said Pop. "*Can* I show you how to light it? I'll say I can! That's the only kind of light we had when I was knee-high to a grasshopper. Now watch! You take off the chimney and turn up the wick, and scratch a match, and presto! there you are!"

"Oh-h-h!" said the girls, as the warm, yellow light began to glow.

They all fell to work with enthusiasm, swept up the kitchen, built a fire in the cookstove, brought in some of their supplies and blankets, and, while Pop stirred up pancakes, the girls made up the bunks for the night.

"I want to sleep in the top bunk," said Eggs. "It's like a train."

"All right, but don't fall out."

"Isn't this fun?" said Eggs. "It's like camping."

"It's more fun than that," said Minty with sudden enthusiasm. "It's really exploring. If we made a camp, that would be our own and we'd know all about it. But this is already made by people we don't know. Everything's strange and we have to explore to find out about it!"

A large living and dining room occupied the center of the house, and on each side of it were curtained doorways which led to four cubbyhole bedrooms. In the rear was a large kitchen with a low, sloping ceiling, too low at the back for either Pop or Minty to stand erect without bumping their heads. One of the bedrooms was apparently used as a storeroom, and in the built-in cupboards, they found linens, blankets, dishes, and knives and forks. The girls selected the largest bedroom for Pop and made up the lower bunk.

"Let's take this next one for ours, Minty," said Eggs. "It looks like a girl's room." Indeed some departed person had succeeded in giving an air of feminine charm to this tiny room. White ruffled curtains were tied back on either side of the window. A triangular shelf, fitted into the corner, had been made into a dressing table by the addition of a looking glass and a petticoat of flowered cretonne. The same flowered cretonne had been used to partition off a small closet, and two delicately tinted wild-flower prints were framed and hung on the wall. A yellow smock and an old brown sweater that were about the right size for Minty hung in the make-shift closet, and a couple of letters stuck behind the mirror were addressed to Miss Marcia Vincent.

"Marcia!" said Minty softly. "Isn't that a lovely name! She must be about my age, and this is her room. Marcia Vincent! How much nicer that sounds than Araminta Sparkes!"

By the time they had finished the beds, wiped off the oilcloth-covered table, and laid out plates, cups, knives and forks, Pop was ready with the pancakes.

"All right, ladies, name your orders," called Pop from the kitchen. "Sockdollagers? Gollwhollickers? Or whales?"

"Whales for mine!" yelled Eggs.

"I'll take gollwhollickers," said Minty. Sockdollagers meant pancakes of the usual size, gollwhollickers were the size of a dinner plate, while a whale filled the griddle and had to be folded in four to fit an ordinary plate. It was a marvel to see Pop flip them over just when the under side had reached the perfect golden brown. With butter and brown sugar syrup Pop's pancakes simply melted in the mouth.

"Pop," said Minty, "I wish you'd teach me how to make pancakes like this."

"When you're eighteen, Minty," said Pop gravely, "I'll divulge my secret recipe. It belonged to your grandmother Sparkes, who had it from her grand-mother, and now your poor dear mother's gone, I'm the only person in the world who knows how to make pancakes like these."

"Then why don't you tell us how now?" insisted Eggs.

"This is the reason why," said Pop. "I can make a success of pancakes, and I kind of like to keep the secret to myself. It's the only thing I have ever been a success at."

"Oh, Pop!" cried the girls, "you mustn't say that!" and they dropped their knives and forks to give him syrupy kisses.

"It's just hard times and the depression that have you licked, Pop."

"Other folks seem to weather the depression," said Pop sadly, "but the longer it goes on, the deeper I seem to sink into it. I always was like that."

"Well, I guess nobody can quote the poets any better than you can, Pop!" said Eggs proudly. "You beat them all at that."

"Here now, Pop, you sit down and let me fry," said Minty. "You must be starved. Will you have a sockdollager, a gollwhollicker, or a whale?"

"Give him some sockdollagers," shouted Eggs. "You know that nobody but Pop can flop a gollwhollicker or a whale."

"That's right, Minty," said Pop more cheerfully. "I'm the only one who can turn a whale. Yes, I'm a success at pancakes!"

Minty looked around the kitchen as she fried Pop's cakes. The low wooden ceilings and walls were brown with age and wood smoke. The pots and pans which

hung about the wall gleamed in the dim yellow light of the lamp. It was warm and secure here. She felt more at home than she had felt for a long time. She thought of the little bedroom with the smock and sweater that were just her size.

"Marcia Vincent," she said softly to herself. "Marcia Vincent—Marcia Vincent." When she carried the last pile of sockdollagers in to Pop, she said suddenly: "Pop, why didn't you give me a pretty name like Marcia? Araminta's such a funny name."

"Well, now, Minty, your mother and I had a good

reason for that. We named you after your great-aunt Araminta, thinking that she might leave you some of her money."

"Did she?" asked Eggs.

"No, it seems the poor old soul had other plans," said Pop. "But Eglantine now—there's a pretty name. Your mother wanted to call you Betty Jean, Eggs, but I said: 'No, my dear. Let's think of something worthy of the poets.' I thought quite a while, and then it came to me— Eglantine! Pure inspiration that was! Yes, and pure poetry, too."

Water steamed cozily in the tea kettle, and, after supper, the two girls set about doing dishes. Pop lighted a fire in the living room fireplace and filled his pipe. Then he pulled up a rocking chair and began to take notice of his surroundings.

"Say, girls," he called, "there're books here! My land! a whole shelf full! Look here! The world's best short stories in ten volumes—and poetry! *The Golden Treasury*, and Shakespeare and Browning, and here's the poet Wordsworth! My stars! girls, there's enough reading here to last a family a whole winter!"

"Well, read all you can tonight, Pop," advised Minty. "We'll be gone tomorrow."

"Books!" said Pop. "Think of that in this wilderness! I guess these are educated people here who know how to enjoy themselves."

"Sure," said Minty, "they're *Marcia's* people!" She already felt a little proprietary thrill in claiming distinction for Marcia's people. Since she had discovered Marcia, she felt as if Marcia somehow belonged to her.

After the dishes were done they all sat around the fire and listened to Pop reading aloud. Even Buster basked in the warmth and sighed happily in his sleep.

"Isn't it nice here?" said Eggs sleepily. "If I had a house like this, I'd live in it."

"I s'pose they've got another house in town somewhere," said Minty.

"Think of having two houses," said Eggs, "and we haven't even got one!"

"We've got Aunt Amy's," said Minty dubiously.

"Oh, Aunt Amy's! Who wants to go there? We all know she doesn't want us!"

"Tut-tut!" said Pop, closing *The Golden Treasury* and pushing his spectacles up on his forehead. "She never really *said* she didn't want us."

"Well, she did everything but yell it from the housetops," said Eggs.

"Now, Eglantine, you mustn't say that," said Pop. "Aunt Amy's letter wasn't so awfully bad, considering everything. Read it again, Minty, and see if it was."

Out of her small, imitation leather handbag, Minty took a letter and slowly unfolded it.

"Do we have to read it again, Pop?" she begged.

"I think we'd better, Minty."

"We were having such a good time," protested Eggs.

"Well, we mustn't forget Aunt Amy's kindness to us," said Pop gloomily. "We'll be there in another day or two, if we can get the car fixed." Both girls sighed, and then Minty began to read:

Minneapolis, Minn.,
Sept. 30.

Dear Charley:
I cannot say that your letter came as a surprise to me. Knowing the way you fail at everything you turn your hand to, I must say I been expecting you to ask me for help any time. Not that it is going to be easy for me to give it to you. My husband and I have all we can do now without shouldering you and your troubles, too. Well, come along, we shall do the best we can for you. You can have the two back bedrooms that I might be letting out to young men with jobs. If it were not for your two girls and the memory of my poor sister who was their mother, I must say, Charley, I'd let you go to the poor house. Of all the no-account, poetry-quoting fools I ever see, you, my dear Charley, are one of the worst. I hope you aren't bringing any pets.
Let me know when you will arrive so I can turn out my lodgers.

Yours truly,
Amy Pearson

"She means to be real kind," said Pop apologetically. "All she says about me is true. She'll be a good aunt to you."

"I don't like her," said Eggs.

"And it's *not* all true what she says about you, Pop," protested Minty. "You haven't been a failure to us."

"I don't know, Minty. I'm afraid I have. Here I can't give you a roof over your heads except a borrowed one."

"But we like you," said Eggs, "and don't forget how you can make gollwhollickers."

"Did you notice what she says about hoping we don't bring any pets?" asked Minty. They all looked mournfully at Buster. Buster got up and laid his head on Pop's knee.

"Buster's a failure too," said Pop almost proudly. "He's got setter's ears and a spitz's tail, a collie's muzzle, and the body of a chow—a little of each and not a success at any one."

"But he's so good!" said Minty. "There never was a better or a smarter dog. I hope Aunt Amy likes him."

"She won't," predicted Eggs. For a moment they sat in gloomy silence. Then Pop sighed deeply and rose.

"Well, kids, let's get to bed."

Suddenly Minty's face brightened. She squeezed Eggs around the waist.

"Anyway tonight," she said, "tonight we're going to sleep in Marcia's bed! Let's play that she invited us!"

"What if she could know we were here?" asked Eggs. "Do you think she'd like it?"

"I'm pretending that she would," said Minty.

As they crept under the covers Eggs said sleepily, "Gee! I wish we didn't have to go on tomorrow. I wish we could stay here all winter!"

Minty didn't say anything, because she knew that they had no business in somebody else's summer cottage, but deep in her heart she thought, "Oh, so do I!"

· 3 ·

A GIRL WITH
BLOND BRAIDS

THE NEXT DAY SPARKLED WITH CLEAR, AUTUMN SUN-
shine. Sky and lake were deeply blue; little waves danced
and glittered; yellow leaves jigged and shivered on the
trees or, loosing their hold, floated gaily away on the
breeze. The squirrels were busy storing their last nuts
and acorns, and flocks of little birds flitted about the
trees noisily discussing their journey south.

Eggs and Buster raced off to explore the beach and
the surrounding woods while Minty finished tidying up
the cottage. Pop looked longingly at the fishing rods
and tackle stored in the spare-room cupboard.

"I'd like mighty well to have you see me catch a
fish, Minty," he said. "It would be real nice to have
some fresh fish for a change. I'm a real good hand at
frying them, too."

"You better see what you can do with the car first," said Minty sensibly.

They had pushed the car to the side of the road the night before, so that no one would bump into it, but apparently their precautions had been unnecessary. Their tracks were the only ones that had marked the road since yesterday's rain.

"It's sure a lonely-looking road," said Minty. "I don't see how we ever got so far off the main highway. We must have taken the wrong turn, back in that last town we went through."

> *"It was roses, roses all the way,*
> *With myrtle mixed in my path like mad,"*

quoted Pop with apparently neither rhyme nor reason. Pop seemed so happy this morning that Minty hadn't the heart to remind him that one didn't lose his way in Wisconsin in October because of the roses and myrtle mixed in the path. "That was the poet Browning that said that, I believe," added Pop. He armed himself with a large monkey wrench and opened the hood of the car. "All right," he said gaily. "Come on, Troubles, Pop will fix you!"

To see Pop advancing on the car in this brisk and confident manner would have put hope into anyone who didn't know him, but Minty heard his cheery whistle and the tapping of the monkey wrench on the engine of the car with grave misgivings. If only Pop's genius for making pancakes might have been extended to tinkering with the car!

By noon Pop had the engine pretty thoroughly taken apart and spread along the side of the road. He had stopped quoting the poets and was wiping the sweat from his brow with grimy hands.

"By golly!" he said. "This is the queerest mix-up I ever saw. Who'd ever have thought of putting a car together like this? I certainly wouldn't! I can't make head or tail of it."

Eggs and Buster arrived at this point and said that they were hungry. Minty opened a can of corned beef, sliced up the meat with Pop's pocket knife and put it between crackers. Everybody sat down about the dismantled car and ate the cracker sandwiches and Buster licked the can.

"Oh, dear!" thought Minty. "It's always like this. Why can't we have a little house of our own and things nice the way they were last night?" Perhaps Pop had been thinking the same thing.

"You know," he said, "I can't possibly finish this thing now today. We might as well plan to stay on another night, and this afternoon I'll do a little fishing. We need something to eat besides canned goods and pancakes. It will save us money in the long run."

So Pop went fishing. The girls helped him dig worms for bait. The boat had been turned upside down on the beach, and the girls helped Pop turn it over and push it into the water. In a very few minutes he had forgotten all about his troubles with the car and that the engine was still lying all along the side of the road. His face shone with delight.

"Spring, the sweet spring, is the year's
pleasant king;
Then blooms each thing, then maids dance
in a ring,
Cold doth not sting, the pretty birds
do sing,
Cuckoo, jug-jug, pu-we, to-witta-woo!"

sang Pop as he rowed the boat out into the lake, and from far out his voice floated back to them: "That's what the poet Nash said."

"Now," said Minty, when he was nearly out of sight, "let's you and me hike along the road and see if we can find anybody who knows how to fix a car."

"Sure," said Eggs. "Maybe there's a house with people in it farther along the road. It will be fun to see."

The road wound pleasantly up and down hill between woods. About a mile farther along they heard the tinkle of cowbells among the trees.

"If there are cows, there must be people," Minty said. Soon they saw open pasture land ahead of them, and across a couple of fields a big red barn and a small white house. Beyond the barn and house they could see a highway where cars occasionally went by.

"That must be the highway we missed yesterday," said Minty. "Gee, I wish—" But did she really wish that they had found it?

Eggs must have had the same thought, for she said, "If we'd been on the right road, Minty, we never would have found Marcia."

24 WINTER COTTAGE

"That's so," said Minty.

As soon as they reached the farmyard Buster saw chickens walking around loose. Buster had been born and reared in Chicago, and this was probably the first time that he had ever beheld a chicken in its natural habitat. He began to bounce up and down and bark. The chickens scattered in every direction, fluttering and squawking, and Buster, now thoroughly delighted, dashed here and there, now after this one, now after that one. At this point a fat, old sheep dog appeared around the house, growling his disapproval. The two girls finally cornered Buster, and Eggs picked him up in her arms. He was almost as big as she was, but Eggs held him firmly, while Minty hurried up to the door and knocked. A mailbox just outside the door bore the name of Mrs. Oscar Gustafson.

A tall, lean woman with light hair came to the door, and behind her appeared the heads of several children. Necessity had made Minty a pretty shrewd judge of character, and as soon as she saw Mrs. Gustafson, some sixth sense told her that she had nothing to fear. Mrs. Gustafson's wide mouth spread pleasantly into an inquiring smile.

"Oh, please," said Minty breathlessly, "is there anyone here who knows how to fix cars? We're stuck down the road a ways, and we're trying to get to Minneapolis to our Aunt Amy's."

"You all alone?" asked Mrs. Gustafson.

"No, our father's with us, but he's not a very good mechanic and so he's gone fishing. I guess we lost our way somehow yesterday."

"How long you been here?"

"Well, we got stuck last night, and Pop's taken the engine all apart, but I'm afraid he won't be able to get it together again. I thought if there was anyone around who understood cars—"

"You been here since last night?" cried Mrs. Gustafson in surprise. "How did you get along?"

Eggs opened her mouth to tell about the Vincent cottage, but Minty said hastily, "We sort of camped—

like. We've got a trailer with food and blankets." She thought it might be just as well not to mention the Vincent cottage, for Mrs. Gustafson might not understand how careful they had been, or that they were going to leave money on the table when they went away.

"Well, come right in," said Mrs. Gustafson. "We're having afternoon coffee. I guess you'll be glad of some too, and I'll send Pete along with you to see what he can do."

Eggs set Buster down inside the kitchen with a box on the ear to put him on his good behavior. She and Minty gratefully received cups of coffee with lots of sugar and rich country cream, and slices of homemade bread still warm from the oven. Eggs was excited.

"I never had coffee before," she stated. "I always wanted to know what it tasted like, but Pop said I was too young. He says it stunts people's growth, but I guess there isn't anything much that can stunt mine. I wear a size twelve-year-old dress now, and a four shoe. I guess that's pretty big for a ten-year-old girl. This coffee is good. I like it." When Eggs had finished this enthusiastic speech, there was silence. Five young Gustafsons looked at her with bright blue eyes and smiling mouths, but nobody said anything. The Gustafsons were quiet folks.

Presently a young man in overalls and a leather jacket unfolded himself from behind the stove, and rose, wiping his mouth with the back of his hand.

"Pete, I want you should go and see what you can

do for these girls and their papa," said Mrs. Gustafson.

"I ain't much of a mechanic," said Pete uncertainly.

"I guess you'll be better than Pop," said Minty.

"You like buttermilk?" inquired the farm woman.

"We never tried any," said Minty.

"Here take this along then. We got more than we can drink." Mrs. Gustafson filled a little tin pail with a thick white liquid full of golden dots of butter.

"Gee! Thank you!" said Minty.

"Your mother's an awfully nice woman," said Eggs to Pete, as they hiked back toward the stranded car.

"Yah," said Pete, and that was all that they could get out of him in the whole mile's walk.

When they reached the car, Pete looked things over silently and then he fell to work. Presently he had everything back where it belonged, and then he got in the car and tried to start it. But it was just as dead as it had been the night before. Pete pushed back his cap and scratched his head. Then he said, "She don't go."

"No, she don't," said Eggs and Minty sympathetically.

"I tell you what you got to do," said Pete. "You got to get a mechanic out from town to tow you in. They charge you about ten dollars to come way out here."

"*Ten dollars!*" said Minty, and she thought to herself, "Why, Pop hasn't got much more than that to take us all the way to Aunt Amy's!"

"If you want I should telephone in for a mechanic—" offered Pete.

"Oh, no!" said Minty. "Not until I've had a chance

to talk to Pop. Maybe he can get it started now that you have put it together. Thank you very much, Mr. Gustafson, and how much do I owe you, please?"

"You don't owe me nothing," said Pete, and he went away down the road whistling a Swedish polka. The "thank you's" which the girls called after him drifted away into the silent woods.

Minty and Eggs went back to the Vincent cottage and built a fire in the cookstove. It already seemed like coming home to be inside again. Minty got some provisions out of the trailer for supper. She was deeply thankful that, when the grocery store failed, they had managed to save enough food to fill the trailer. Surely Aunt Amy could not be too angry with them for coming if they brought enough groceries to see them through the winter. While Minty worked in the kitchen, Eggs went exploring around the cottage again.

"Look what I've found, Minty," she called. "It's a picture of Marcia!" Minty left her cooking and ran to look.

Fastened up with thumbtacks in the unoccupied bedroom was an enlarged snapshot of a young girl, and scrawled across the bottom in a girl's handwriting were the words "Love to Mother from Marcia." Eggs and Minty leaned close to look. The picture was dim but very glamorous. The girl was slender and tall, dressed in a long white dress, and long blond braids hung down on either side of her face. She looked like a princess in a fairy tale instead of an ordinary girl like Minty or Eggs.

"Isn't she pretty?" said Eggs. "Look at her hair! Yellow and long, like Rapunzel or Goldilocks."

"But she's Marcia," said Minty softly. "*Marcia Vincent!*"

Just then there was a shout from the lake, and Pop was landing and pulling the boat up onto the sand. His cheeks were red, his mustache bristled, and his chest seemed several inches larger around than it had been when he went out. He held up two big northern pike.

"*Cuckoo, jug-jug, pu-we, to-witta-woo!*" caroled Pop.

Yes, Pop knew how to fry fish, too! Never were fish fried to a more golden brown, crisp on the outside and tender white within. They tasted marvelous.

After supper Minty told Pop about the car and Pete Gustafson, and how much it would cost to get a mechanic out from town. Pop didn't seem as much disturbed as she had expected him to be.

"You know, girls," he said, "I've been thinking a lot this afternoon. That's one of the nice things about fishing, it gives you plenty of time to think. Well, I thought like this: Your Aunt Amy has still got her lodgers and we haven't written to say when we'll arrive. Now here's a nice empty house with about everything we need in it, why don't we stay here?"

"But, Pop, it doesn't belong to us."

"I know, Minty, but it's too bad to have a good house standing empty. It never did any house good to stand empty all winter. If these folks knew they had a chance to rent it to us, they'd be tickled to death."

"Rent it?" asked the girls.

"Yes, we'll rent it for the winter."

"But where'll you get the money, Pop?"

"Well, I haven't figured that out yet," said Pop. "My ideas come to me one at a time. But we've got all winter to think this thing out. By spring we'll have thought of a good way to earn some money, and we'll leave it in a fruit jar on the table with a note telling them how long we were here and what a good time we had. It'll be just so much velvet for them to have that extra money that they weren't expecting."

"And we wouldn't have to go to Aunt Amy's until spring?" shouted Eggs.

"That's the way I figure it," said Pop.

"Whoopee!" yelled Eggs. Minty didn't say anything, but, as she mixed Buster's supper and scraped the plates, her mind was busy. To have a house like this all winter, all to themselves, without Aunt Amy's grudging charity! How wonderful that would be. Marcia's house! But then how would they ever get money enough for the rent? Minty knew in advance that by spring Pop and Eggs would probably have forgotten all about the rent, and that wouldn't be fair. No, it wouldn't be right to live here if they couldn't pay rent! Marcia wouldn't do a thing like that, Minty knew.

She took the kerosene lamp into the bedroom and held it close to the enlarged snapshot so that she could see Marcia's face again. No, Marcia Vincent wouldn't live in somebody else's house without paying rent for it! She wasn't that kind of girl.

Minty squared her shoulders. "What kind of a girl am *I*?" she wondered. "Pop and Eggs won't worry, but I must. Somehow I'll have to see that the rent gets paid to the Vincents. Somehow."

· 4 ·

THE CONTEST
MAGAZINE

ONCE THEY HAD DECIDED TO STAY IN THE VINCENT COT-
tage, Pop and the girls fell to work with enthusiasm.
The next morning they unloaded the trailer, brought in
the extra clothing and bedding and the groceries which
were to have been a peace offering to Aunt Amy.

"Yes," said Pop, swinging a bag of flour to his shoulder, "we'll make out pretty well here. We'll have to
be careful, of course, and not waste anything. After
all, what we needed most was a roof over our heads."

"Say, Pop," said Eggs while they were unloading,
"do you want to make some money?"

"I'll say I do!" said Pop. Eggs held out a dog-eared
magazine that she had fished out of the bottom of the
trailer.

"It's a contest magazine," she said. "Somebody left
it at that last tourist camp in Eau Claire. I stuck it be-

hind the cracker boxes until I'd have more time to look at it."

"Why should they have a magazine full of contests?" asked Minty.

"Well," Pop said, "everybody needs money these days. Maybe the best way to sell things is to offer prizes for buying what they have to sell."

"It sounds kind of silly," Minty said.

"But, look," said Eggs, "all you have to do to win a prize is tell why you like something, or you add a line to a poem. Hey, Pop, you could add a line to a poem, couldn't you?"

Pop set down the flour, adjusted his spectacles, and looked over Eggs's shoulder.

"A thousand dollars for a slogan for a complexion soap!" he cried. "My, golly! what a lot of money!" Minty joined them and looked over Eggs's other shoulder.

" 'Add a last line to a limerick and win one hundred dollars'!" she read. "That sounds easy. There must be a catch in it somewhere."

"Look here!" cried Eggs. "Here's a perfume company that will give you a pony if you solve this easy puzzle. Think of it, Minty. Think of having a pony!"

"Where could we keep it?" asked Minty doubtfully.

"Well," began Eggs, who hadn't thought that far ahead, "of course we could have them send it on to Aunt Amy's—" Their faces all went a little sour at the recollection of Aunt Amy.

"I expect Aunt Amy doesn't like ponies," said Minty finally.

Pop managed to get the sack of flour into the kitchen, but then he and Eggs stopped work for an hour and devoted themselves to the contest magazine.

"Here we have the winter before us," cried Pop, "and all of those contests just waiting to be solved! Eglantine, you plucked a jewel from that trash heap. Why, we ought to be rolling in wealth by spring. Eh, Minty?"

"Maybe so," said Minty, struggling in with the last things from the trailer. "I certainly hope so! But it sounds awfully easy—too good to be true. And now we better get back to work."

There were plenty of things to do to get ready for winter before the first snows came. Down at one side of the cottage they discovered a big pile of dead wood and brush that had been cleared out of the woods during the summer. Pop found an ax and a saw in the woodshed, and he set out to cut the oak, birch, and poplar logs into stove-length pieces which the girls piled in the shed. Pop was an excellent worker when his interest was aroused.

"We'll need a lot of fuel to keep us warm all winter, girls," he said. "You go out into the woods and bring in every bit of dead, dry wood you can find, and anything else you find that might be useful."

The sun continued to shine all that week, and Minty whistled as she worked, feeling happier than she had ever felt in all her life before. The air was cold in spite of the sun, and it seemed to sparkle as the little waves sparkled on the lake. The girls ran hither and thither,

hauling in broken branches and fallen logs. At night they were tired, but each day had been fun.

Eggs discovered a hazel copse which was still well stocked with nuts in spite of the busy squirrels, and the girls brought pails and baskets from the house and gathered the nuts. Across the lake in a swamp, wild cranberries still hung like red fairy balloons suspended by threads from the low brush. Pop rowed the girls over one day, and they gathered all they could find. Later, with much good advice from Eggs and Pop, Minty stewed the cranberries with sugar and sealed them away in some of the empty fruit jars which she found on a shelf in the kitchen.

At this time of year the woods were full of mushrooms. Besides knowing so much about the English

poets, Pop had somewhere picked up a surprising knowl-
edge of mushrooms.

"What if you got some poison mushrooms by mistake, Pop?" asked Minty.

"Why, Minty, I've never made a mistake yet," he
said pleasantly. "So while the mushroom season lasts,
we might as well eat all we can and save the canned
beef and sardines for the middle of winter. I sure do
like living off the land."

"Pop," said Minty, "what if Marcia's people should
come back for something?"

"We'd say 'Surprise!' and give them a nice dish of
fish chowder, and then we'd move out. Maybe they
could tell us how to start our car. Minty, you do beat
all for worrying."

"I can't help it," Minty said.

"She's *sus*-picious," said Eggs, "that's what Minty
is. She's *sus*-picious."

Minty was provoked. "Somebody has to be suspicious
in this family," she retorted. "I'm sorry I'm the one.
But you and Pop—why, you'd just trade your last dollar
for wooden nickels if anybody asked you to."

"Wooden nickels!" Eggs was interested. "I never saw
a wooden nickel, Minty. What are they like?"

"I never saw one either," said Minty more mildly,
"but they're something like the beans Jack gave away
his cow for, I guess."

"Well, Jack did all right for himself," Eggs said. "He
got this talking harp and the goose that laid the golden
eggs and all the giant's treasure. Why aren't wooden
nickels any good?"

"Oh, bother!" said Minty. "It's no use trying to explain."

"Minty's all right," said Pop. "She's got a real level head on her shoulders. You and me could take a lesson from Minty, Eglantine, and don't let us forget it."

After Pop had spent his morning chopping wood, he usually took Eggs fishing with him for the afternoon. Now that they had discovered the contest magazine they took that with them and solved puzzles or made up slogans while they fished. Minty usually had work to do around the cottage, for she considered herself chief housekeeper, and she took a stern pride in "keeping Marcia's house nice." It was such fun to have a house to keep—after all the dreary rented rooms they had lived in during the past two years!

Sometimes she went to the stream and knelt on the bank and looked at the leafy brown clearness of it as it ran over round stones. The sound of the running water filled her ears with music, and she wanted to sing with it. Sometimes, when she and Buster rambled through the woods, there would be a sudden sharp whirring of wings and a covey of partridges would thunder away through the brush. At first Minty was frightened, and then she was delighted. This was a brand-new world to her. One day, when Buster had gone panting and snuffling in the opposite direction on the trail of a squirrel, Minty came out through the woods to the lake shore. She was walking quietly against the wind, and on the far shore, across a little stretch of water, she saw a deer, which had come down to drink. For a full moment she watched it, before it turned and disappeared in the woods, its white tail bobbing like a beacon over fallen logs.

One evening Minty thought of something.

"What about school, Pop?" Pop and Eggs both looked surprised, and Eggs said:

"Oh, Minty! Why bring that up?"

"That's true!" said Pop. "Minty, you do have a monumental brain. To remember that! It clean slipped my mind! Of course, you and Eglantine should be going to school. But how can you, way out here? Well, a winter's vacation won't do you any harm, and, anyway, look at all the books they have here! You can read all those, and I guess it'll be every bit as good as school."

"And no arithmetic and geography?" shouted Eggs.

"Well, not so you could notice," said Pop apologetically.

"Whoopee!"

"It's like this," said Pop. "If we win all these contests I'm figuring on, we'll be well off by spring. We'll get the car fixed up—or win a better one—and I'll drive you into town and put you in a nice boarding school, and then you can catch up on the arithmetic and geography."

"Oh, Pop!" cried Minty. "You know all that will never happen!"

"*How* do I know?" asked Pop. "It might, mightn't it?"

Minty was tired of making objections. "Well, it suits me," she said, looking around the cozy, firelit room.

"Which contest are you going to try first, Pop?"

"There's the Spring Field Butter Contest," said Pop dreamily. "They want a poem to advertise their butter. I think I've got a mighty good one. They'll pay a thousand dollars for the best one, and a lot of other prizes down to a dollar for the hundred and fifth prize."

> *"Butter, butter,*
> *Slick an' yellow,*
> *Gosh! but how*
> *It fills a fellow!"*

shouted Eggs. "Look, Pop, I've made one! Do you s'pose they'd give me a prize?"

"No, Eglantine. They want something dignified and elegant—something with poetic beauty. I thought of this one:

> *"The curfew tolls the knell of parting day,*
> *The lowing herds wind slowly o'er the lea,*
> *And each fair cow that plods its weary way*
> *Is bringing Spring Field Butter home to me."*

"Why, Pop, that's Gray's 'Elegy in a Country Churchyard'," exclaimed Minty.

"Not the part about Spring Field Butter," protested Pop. "That's my own. But who am I to write nobler verse than Thomas Gray? I ask you that, Minty. Spring Field Butter wants the best poem it can get, and there you have it. You write it out for me, Minty. You can write a nice clear hand, and I see they've left us paper and ink."

"They've left some stamps here, too, Pop," she said, exploring the shelf. "There are a whole lot of them but they are all stuck together."

"I'll steam them apart," said Pop, "and you can charge them up to the rent account."

"What address shall I put on the poem?" asked Minty. They looked at her in surprise.

"Address?"

"Yes, the postman doesn't come out this road. The Vincents have a letter box at the Gustafsons' farm, and the Gustafsons don't know we are living here. I expect they think we've gone on by now."

"I declare, Minty," said Pop. "You do think of everything!"

"We could give Aunt Amy's address, I suppose."

"No, no, that wouldn't do, because, if we get the prize, we ought to have it before we leave here—or else how are we going to pay our rent and get the car fixed?"

"That's so. I'll tell you, Pop. I'll put your address, R.F.D., Scandian Corners, Wisconsin, care of Mrs. Oscar Gustafson. I don't expect the prize will come very soon if it comes at all, and the Gustafsons will have to find out sometime that we are spending the winter here."

"You needn't be ashamed of it, Minty," said Pop. "I'm an honest man, and I'm renting this house for the winter, and you can tell the Gustafsons so, if they ask you."

"All right," said Minty. "But what if they wrote to the Vincents?"

"Well, I'd tell the Vincents so, too. They couldn't do worse than turn us out."

Pop sneezed and stretched his arms up over his head.

"I guess I'll turn in, girls," he said. "I don't feel so fancy tonight. It must have been sitting so long out there on the lake today. Those fish were mighty slow to bite and the cold sort of went all through my bones. How are you, Eggs?"

"Fine, Pop."

"That's good. Well, goodnight, girls. *To sleep! perchance to dream! Ay, there's the rub.* That's what the—"

"—poet Shakespeare said," shouted Minty and Eggs. "Good night, Pop."

· 5 ·

STRANGER
ON THE ROAD

THE NEXT DAY A COLD RAIN BEAT AGAINST THE WINDOWS
and a cold wind rattled the doors. Yellow and brown
leaves flew with the wind and left the trees bare skele-
tons with arms upraised to the gray sky. The beautiful
blue lake had turned a heavy gray, and uneasy white-
caps bobbed upon it and flung themselves with threat-
ening thunder on the beach. It was an exciting day.
Minty and Eggs, in their old raincoats, dashing to the
beach to see that the boat was fast, running to the stream
for water, or snatching dry wood from the woodshed,
flung up their arms and capered. They shouted, and the
wind took their shouts and bore them away like nothing.

But Pop stayed indoors all day, hugging the fire and
sneezing, his cheeks unusually red and his eyes bright.
By night he was coughing, and complaining that he

ached in all his bones. Minty heated water for his feet, made him a cup of tea, and put him to bed with an extra covering of blankets.

Of course it was only a cold, but somehow Minty felt frightened. What would they do if any of them became seriously ill? They were all alone here, with no telephone, no car, no friends to call upon. They couldn't afford to hire a doctor out from town and their only medicines consisted of a small emergency kit and a sample of stomach pills which someone had once given Pop. What could they do if one of them fell sick?

As Minty lay in bed that night, thinking, the wind beat against the cottage like heavy wings. Wet leaves flew against the windows and the trees creaked and groaned. Under the kitchen she could hear the woodchucks scurrying and scratching and squeaking among themselves. She thought of all the little frightened, hunted things that scurry about in storm-swept forests, and it seemed to her tonight that she was one of them.

Resolutely she turned her mind to something safe and pleasant. She would think of Marcia Vincent, who was safe and sheltered and secure. Marcia had slept in this very bed. There *were* girls like Marcia in the world! But, with the wind howling and the waves beating outside, the thought of Marcia Vincent's plenty was not very comforting to Minty.

The next day Pop was much worse. He tossed and groaned and seemed to have no appetite for the food which Minty prepared. This wasn't like Pop, and the two girls looked at each other with frightened eyes.

"Just a cold," said Pop. "Don't worry, I'll be up tomorrow." But late in the afternoon he grew worse, and began quoting poetry and discussing the price of vegetables and coffee in a queer voice to no one in particular, and then he said, "Come, Mable, I'll help you with the dishes and we'll take the kids to the movies."

"He's gone clean out of his head, Minty," said Eggs in a frightened whisper. "He thinks he's talking to Mother."

"Somebody's got to go for Mrs. Gustafson," said Minty. "Put on your things, Eggs."

"Oh, Minty, I'm scared to go alone. I'll stay here with Pop and you go."

"All right. But you must keep him covered and keep the fire up."

Minty flung on her wrap and ran out of doors. The storm of the day and night before was over, and everything lay gray and silent under a heavy sky. The trees dripped, and wet leaves were deep and rustling underfoot.

All that Minty could think of was getting Mrs. Gustafson to help her with Pop. The Gustafsons would be angry with them for staying in a cottage that didn't belong to them. Perhaps they would write to the Vincents and tell them. But it couldn't be helped. Pop was sick and Minty didn't know what to do. Mrs. Gustafson would know.

Minty ran until she was out of breath; then she walked

quickly, her hand pressed to her aching side. Poor Pop! it was awful to hear him mixing up poetry and groceries in that senseless way and talking to Mother as if she were still here!

At last there was the tinkle of cowbells and the lightness of open sky and pasture land. Just across the fields was the barn and the little white house.

When she reached the back porch, Minty clung to the post for a moment to catch her breath. She hadn't thought what she would say. It had seemed as if Mrs. Gustafson would understand without having to be told. As she stood there panting, she heard running feet in the kitchen and a burst of laughter. Then someone began to sing in a language which she did not understand, and there were more shouts of laughter.

"Oh, they are having a party!" thought Minty in despair. But still she went up to the door and knocked. A small boy flung it wide, and inside Minty saw a girl kneeling down to test a cake in the open oven. A smaller girl was laying the table and several little boys of assorted sizes were having a good-natured rough-and-tumble fight on a lounge in the corner. The lamp was already lighted and it was a gay and cheerful scene.

The moment the door opened the children all stopped what they were doing and gazed at Minty in silence with wondering blue eyes.

"Oh, please," cried Minty desperately, "is your mother at home?"

The largest girl closed the oven door and came to look at Minty, with her hands on her hips, her eyes as blue and wondering as the children's. "You still here?" she said. "We thought you'd gone."

"No," said Minty. "I want to see your mother. I've got to see her."

"Mom isn't here," said the girl. "She's gone by her sister's up to Superior for a week. Her sister's sick."

"Oh, so is my pop," said Minty.

"Too bad. Mom is sure good with sick people. We miss her. I got my hands full with these kids, I tell you." The girl waved a hand toward the roomful of motionless children, all ready to leap into action again when the stranger should be gone.

"Oh," said Minty again. "I see."

"Yah, I sure got my hands full all right," the girl repeated. "What was you wanting?"

"Oh, I wanted your mother—I wanted—"

Suddenly one of the younger children fell off of a rocking chair and began to howl. As if at a signal the remaining silent and staring children burst into noise and motion. The kitchen rocked with their shouts. The older girl put her hands to her ears and shouted to Minty, "What did you say you wanted?"

"Nothing," said Minty. "Nothing! I guess you couldn't help me."

"Now you kids behave yourselves!" shouted the Gustafson girl.

The door closed. The air was silent and cold. Blind with disappointment, Minty turned and ran back the way she had come. She had crossed the pasture and was in the dark woods again before her mind began to clear. "I might have asked the girl for help," she thought. "Maybe she would have known what to do. But it didn't look like it. She said her hands were full and I could see it was so. Oh, what shall I do now?"

She began to walk more slowly. Everything seemed unfriendly today. The sky was a sullen gray, the branches were bare, and the fallen leaves beneath her feet were stiff with frost. They made a scuffling noise as she walked. Suddenly it seemed to her that feet other than hers were rustling the frosty leaves. Around the next bend she saw that someone was coming along the road ahead of her.

Minty dashed the tears out of her eyes and squared her shoulders. Misty twilight was already gathering in the woods and Minty couldn't see who was coming, but he looked about the size of Pete Gustafson. At that Minty's heart leaped. Pete had put the car together, perhaps he could help with Pop. But as the boy came nearer she saw that he was smaller than Pete and more sturdily built. He had a gun on his arm and a couple of partridges were tied by their necks to the belt of his mackinaw. His high boots were caked with mud and he had a packsack on his back. His cap was pulled well down over his eyes. He drew to one side of the narrow road as she came along and would have pushed by her hurriedly without looking at her, but Minty cried desperately:

"Oh, stop!"

"I don't have to," said the boy in a gruff voice, without either looking at her or slowing his pace.

"Oh, yes, you do, too!" cried Minty, catching his arm.

"Why? Are these your woods?" At last the boy had stopped and was looking at her. His face was sullen and defiant.

"Yes," said Minty desperately. "They are our woods."

"Well, take your old partridges then! I can do without them." With a fierce wrench he broke the string that fastened the partridges to his belt and held them out to her.

"But I don't want partridges," gasped Minty.

"Go on. Tell the game warden, if you want to. It

can't hurt me. I'll be out of the county by morning."

"Oh, listen!" said Minty. "I don't know anything about partridges or game wardens. My pop's sick, and we haven't any medicines or anything, and Eggs and I are all alone, and I don't know what to do. Do you know anything about doctoring?"

"What if I do?" the boy asked defensively.

He looked at her in silence for a moment, and gradually his face changed as if a fixed idea were giving way to something new and unexpected. The look of surly defiance changed to one of mild surprise, but he was still suspicious.

"How do I know your pop's sick?"

"Well, you can come and see. I'm not lying to you— except when I said we owned these woods. I just said that to get you to stop. We don't own anything." The boy still stood in the road and looked at her, the dead partridges hanging from his outstretched hand.

"Oh, you *are* dumb!" cried Minty with something like a sob. "I guess *you* can't help me either. We're out of luck, as usual. Take your old partridges and get out of the county by morning if you want to."

"I'm not so dumb as you think. What's the matter with your pop?"

"Why, he caught a cold, and now he's terribly feverish, and he's gone clean out of his head and talking nonsense."

"Where do you live?"

"Just back here in the woods a bit. Will you come?"

"Yes, I'll come."

"Oh, thanks! I'll show you the way. My name's Minty Sparkes. What's yours?" The look of suspicion returned to the boy's eyes.

"You got a radio?"

"No."

"How long you been here?"

"About two weeks. Why?"

"Oh, nothing. I'll tell you my name. It's Joe Boles."

· 6 ·

THERE'S A DOCTOR
IN THE HOUSE

IN THE LAMPLIGHT OF THE COTTAGE JOE BOLES APPEARED
to be about sixteen, sturdily built, with a square, determined chin, a sullen lower lip, and clear gray eyes,
set wide apart. As soon as he entered the cottage, Minty
felt that he had taken charge. He tossed the partridges
onto the table and said:

"You can cook those things if you want to." Then
he eased the packsack off his back, placed it on a chair,
and opened it with a businesslike air.

"I'd like some hot water, please, and soap and a clean
towel," he said. Minty flew to obey, while Eggs stood
by in openmouthed astonishment. Presently Eggs ran
to the kitchen, where Minty was assembling the hot
water, soap, and towel.

"Is he a real doctor, Minty?" she whispered.

"No, he's just a boy I met on the road. Mrs. Gustafson was away."

"But he's got a real doctor's bag. He took it out of his knapsack."

Minty came to the living room door to look. Sure enough, beside the partridges and the gun, Joe Boles had laid out a well-worn leather medical kit, such as country doctors carry on their rounds. He opened it in a professional manner and Minty saw rows of tiny bottles, a few tools, and a stethoscope.

"How about that hot water?" he asked in a business-like voice.

"Coming right away," said Minty.

Joe washed his hands with the greatest of care. If the truth be told, they needed it sorely, but Joe worked at them until they were as clean as a doctor's. Then he took his medical kit and went into Pop's room. Minty held the light for him, and Eggs stood by in considerable awe. Pop was lying a little more quietly now, but he still mumbled snatches of Wordsworth and Browning mingled with the price of celery and the number of boxes of cereal to be stocked.

Joe sterilized a thermometer in a small bottle of alcohol, rinsed it in water, shook it down, and put it in Pop's mouth. Then he drew out a cheap watch with a noisy tick and carefully took Pop's pulse. Pop opened his eyes and they seemed to clear themselves of the fog that had been hovering in them all afternoon.

"Are you the doctor?" he asked weakly.

"Yes, sir, I'm the doctor," said Joe Boles. "You're going to be all right now. Just let me listen to your

heart and lungs a minute." He put the ends of the
stethoscope into his ears and went carefully over Pop's
chest. "M-hm," he said at last, straightening himself
and taking the stethoscope out of his ears. He consulted
the labels on two or three of the small bottles in his
case. Was he undecided, or just being important? At
last he shook out two small white tablets in his hand,
and made Pop take them with a drink of water. Then he
turned to Minty.

"Do you have any onions?"

"Oh, yes, we have onions."

"Do you know how to make an onion poultice?"

"No, I don't think so."

"Well, here, get me the onions and I'll make you one."

In about fifteen minutes Joe had a most unholy-smell-
ing mess of half-cooked onions spread between old
pieces of torn sheet, and laid hot on Pop's chest. Pop
opened his eyes with a glimmer of consciousness.

"My golly!" he said in a weak voice. "It ought to
kill or cure."

"I know it smells pretty strong, sir," said Joe, "but
it'll fix you right up. Try to go to sleep now. And you,
Minty, open up his window, so he gets some air."

"Do you really think he'll be all right now?" asked
Minty, when they were in the living room again.

"I've done the best I could," said Joe. "I guess he
will."

"It was awfully kind of you. I don't know how to
thank you."

"I've got a good appetite," said Joe.

"All right. I'll fix you some supper right away, and

you better plan to stay the night. There's an extra
bedroom, and it's a long way to the nearest house, or
do you live around here?"

"No, I don't live around here."

"Then, if Pop should get worse, you'd be here handy."
For the first time a kind of crooked smile broke the
professional seriousness of Joe's manner.

"Yes," he said, "I'd kind of like to see this case
through." Then he looked around suspiciously. "There
aren't any other folks staying here, are there? Are
you all alone?"

"Yes, we're all alone."

"All right," said Joe. "I'll stay. Here, let me show
you how to skin those partridges. I was kind of counting on them for supper, but I didn't aim to cook them
on a stove."

"Where *did* you aim to cook them?" asked Eggs, who
had scarcely taken her eyes from Joe Boles's face since
the moment he arrived.

"Oh, on a spit over a little fire," said Joe carelessly.
His hands moved quickly and efficiently, stripping the
feathers from the wild birds. With no fumbling or
wasted motion, he slit them open and drew and cleaned
them.

"Here's some feathers for your doll's hats," he said.

"I've got a doll named Peacharino," Eggs said, "but
she don't have a hat. Say, if you eat out of doors, where
do you sleep?"

"Outdoors."

"Isn't it cold?"

"Yep, it's cold. But I like it."

"Haven't you got a home?"

"Say, does this kid ever do anything but ask questions?" asked Joe, the crooked smile hovering about his lips again.

"Yes, she sets the table," said Minty, putting some knives and forks into Eggs's hands.

Pop spent a restless and uncomfortable night, and at intervals Joe took his pulse or listened to his lungs with the stethoscope, renewing the poultice or shaking out small white tablets from the bottle in the medicine kit as they were needed. Neither Joe nor Minty went to bed, but kept up the fire in the fireplace, and sat quietly on either side of it listening for Pop's cough or call. Joe did not seem to want to talk, but Minty could see that he liked to keep his hands busy. He carefully selected a smooth piece of birch wood and began to whittle and shape it with his pocket knife. He was in no hurry to finish it, but worked with patience and care, and at last Minty could see that it was going to be a squirrel sitting up and holding a nut.

She had the comfortable feeling that the responsibility of Pop's illness had been taken off her shoulders, and that someone wiser than she was now in charge. She was tired out by the emotion and worry of the past day, and it was wonderful to have someone who seemed to know what to do come in and take charge.

"Gee! but I was lucky!" she thought to herself. "To think that the first person I met on the road was a doctor! Of course, he's awfully young, but he *must* be a doctor—he's got all the fixings."

Minty's head began to nod, and the next thing she

knew daylight was coming in the window and she was feeling very stiff and cramped from sleeping in a rocking chair. But she was not cold, for the fire was still burning and someone had covered her with a blanket while she slept. Joe Boles was in the kitchen, frying bacon and making coffee. Pop's voice, like the croak of a tired frog, came out of his bedroom.

"Do I smell coffee? I sure could do with a cup right now. And, say, somebody take this awful-smelling Irish stew off my chest!"

Minty yawned and stretched, and her eyes traveled dazedly about the room. At last they came to rest on the center of the mantelpiece, where there was something which she had not seen the night before. It was Joe Boles's squirrel, neatly finished and perfect in every detail.

· 7 ·

CONFESSIONS

POP WAS SITTING UP BY THE FIREPLACE IN TWO OR THREE days' time, and Joe Boles was still with them. At first Joe had had to make up some of the sleep he had lost before starting out again, and then he had been sincerely interested in Pop's case and wanted to be sure that he was quite well before he left. One afternoon he took the fishing tackle and caught them enough fish for supper.

"Are you folks really planning to stay here all winter?" he asked.

"Yes, we are," said Minty.

"Well, you sure need to have a lot of things done before you do."

"I guess we do," said Minty. "We have to split up a lot more wood, I know."

"You sure do," said Joe, "and you'd be a lot warmer if you had some dirt banked up around the foundation of the house, and a few boards nailed on where they've come loose." And Joe spent another day nailing loose boards, banking the foundation, and splitting wood.

"We can't pay you much," said Minty, "because we haven't got much. This house isn't even ours. Of course, we're renting it, but I don't know yet where the rent money is coming from. We're just nothing at all."

"That's all right," said Joe. "I'm not looking for pay. I'm nothing at all myself. But someday I will be somebody. I've made up my mind to that."

"It's nice to be so sure," said Minty.

"You've got to be sure. Things don't happen unless you make them." Joe shut his mouth in a grim line and went on chopping wood.

That night Pop was almost his old self again. On one of the shelves in the living room he had found a box of chessmen and a board, and he had made the discovery that Joe Boles played chess. After supper they drew up a table before the fire and began to play.

"Joe," said Pop, "you're a wonderful boy. I don't know how you happened along here, or where you came from, but you certainly saved my life." Joe smiled his uneasy smile.

"Oh, I guess you'd have pulled through all right without me," he said. "I just came along at the right time and did what I could."

"Nevertheless, Joe, I'm sincerely grateful to you for saving my life."

"Well, Mr. Sparkes," said Joe, "I'm grateful to you for living. It would have been pretty hard on me if you had died. You see, you were my first case."

"Your *first* case?"

"That's right."

"But, Joe," cried Eggs, "you acted just like a real doctor!"

"Oh, I know how they act," said Joe. "My father was a doctor and someday I'm going to be one like him. That's his medicine kit I've got."

"But the pills and the poultice!" cried Minty. "You certainly knew just what to do." Joe blushed and pushed the chessmen aside.

"The pills were just aspirin," he said, "and that poultice—well, I guess a doctor would probably laugh at that. But I couldn't think what else to do. I remember my grandmother used to make them like that and put them on people when they had congested chests. Dad used to laugh at her. But she would say, 'Old women's recipes are often as good as your newfangled ones, Doctor.' Someday I'll know a better way of curing congested chests than that."

"Well, it's a marvel to me," said Pop. "I don't care how that poultice smelled, it certainly did the work. *A rose by any other name would smell as sweet*, as the poet Shakespeare says. I think you'll make a wonderful doctor, Joe. You've got a splendid bedside manner."

"Thanks," said Joe. "I wish I had about eight years of medical training."

"Oh, that will come," said Pop optimistically.

"Will it? I wonder. It doesn't look much like it now."

"Things don't happen unless you make them," said Minty suddenly. Joe's words had been going through her mind all afternoon and now she tossed them back at him. He gave her one of his rare smiles.

"That's so," he said. "But, honestly, I've had a hard row to hoe."

"Joe," said Pop, looking keenly at the boy, "your father was a doctor and your grandmother was a smart woman. It sounds to me like you had a fine family. How come you're out here all alone, shooting partridges out of season for your food, and sleeping out of doors in October?"

"I'm heading for the South."

"Yes, but that family of yours, where are they?"

"I haven't got a family anymore," said Joe. The sullen look had settled onto his face again. "I had one once, but it's all broken up now, and what's left of it I'm trying to forget."

"I guess you've run away from home," said Pop calmly. Joe's face went fiery red.

"What makes you say that?" he cried.

"You look like a boy who'd do a darn fool thing like that, Joe."

Joe clenched his hands, "Well, are you going to notify the police?"

"No," said Pop, "not unless you write and tell Aunt Amy where *we* are. You see, Joe, we're hiding out on a family too. This is a pretty good place to do it."

"I'll say it's a good place to hide," said Joe. "Why, you can go fifty miles off to the east of here and you won't even find a settler's shack. This country is where the gangsters hide out when they get in trouble in Chicago."

"Gangsters?" cried Eggs, all excited.

"Don't you know what gangsters are?" asked Joe.

"Sure I know what gangsters are," exclaimed Eggs. She made her two index fingers into imaginary guns. "Stick 'em up, podner," she said. "Ack-ack-ack-ack-ack!"

"Yes," said Pop, "Amy would have a pretty hard time locating us up here."

"Aunt Amy wouldn't waste much time in hunting.

She don't like pets," said Eggs, hugging Buster around the neck.

"You know, they broadcast over the radio for me," said Joe almost proudly. "I heard them in a grocery store where I went to buy some grub. I've stayed away from towns since then."

"You didn't run away from your father or your grandmother, Joe—I know that," said Pop. "Who did you run away from?"

"No, they're both dead. My father died two years ago in an automobile accident. One day he was there, the next he was gone . . ." Joe's voice trailed off.

Pop took off his spectacles and polished them. "Well?" he said.

"Well," said Joe, "that left just my mother and me, and we got along pretty well until last summer." Joe paused again, and then he said in a hard voice, "Last summer she got married again."

"I guess you didn't like your new father very well," prompted Pop.

"Like him?" said Joe fiercely. "I hate him, and he hates me. He tries to make me do things. He isn't like my dad. I can't live there anymore. I packed my things and got out. They'll never make me go back—no, never! I'll die first!"

Eggs and Minty looked at Joe with round eyes. Everyone was silent for a moment. They could hear the crackle of wood on the fire and the whisper of wind outside, and it almost seemed that they could hear the whisper and crackle of Joe's anger, too. They could see

that Joe did not love or hate easily and quietly. Things
went deep with him. At last Pop began to put the chessmen back in the box, and he asked calmly:

"What do you figure on doing now, Joe?"

"I don't know," said Joe. "I just want to get away
south where I don't have to freeze out of doors at night,
and, when I'm safe away where they won't bring me
back, I want to get a job, so I can go to school again
someday and learn to be a doctor like my dad. But I
don't know why I've told you all this. I guess it's
because I'll be on my way again tomorrow, and you
can forget all about it."

"Joe," said Pop, "if I had the money, I'd hire you to
stay here and see us through the winter. I'm not very
strong and it puts too much work on Minty and Eggs.
We need the strong arm of that son I never had. But
there's no use talking about that. All I could give you
to pay for your help would be your board, and a room
in a borrowed summer cottage. I guess that wouldn't
get you very far on the way to being a doctor in a
hurry, would it? Well, we'll have to get along without
you. But like you said, this place is remote. If gangsters
can hide out here, I guess we can too. I don't s'pose
they'd ever think of tracing any of us out here. This
place is cozy and cheerful, too. I look forward to quite
a nice winter here with books and chess and a little
hunting and fishing. A place like this sort of puts a
man on his mettle. If I were twenty years younger, I'd
enjoy it more. But you'll be off by yourself, riding the
rails and hitting the trails. I guess it's pretty cold now

riding under a freight train. But you're young. You
can do it." Pop rose and stretched. His legs were still
a little wobbly. "Well, good night all. What was it
the poet Shakespeare said, girls?"

"To sleep! Perchance to dream! Ay, there's the rub!"
shouted Eggs. Minty followed her father into his room.

"Pop," she whispered, "why didn't you urge him to
stay here?"

"You go to sleep, Minty," said Pop, patting her head.
"We'll see what he says in the morning."

Pop arose with the rest of them the next morning.
He was still pale and a little weak in the knees, but
some inner purpose stiffened his back. With unusual
care he mixed up a batch of his famous pancakes, and
never in the history of the family had such perfect sockdollagers and gollwhollickers been made as Pop made
that morning. Golden brown, dripping with butter and
syrup, they melted on the tongue.

"Say!" said Joe. "These are sure the best hot cakes
I ever tasted."

"Nothing much," said Pop modestly. "Just an old
family recipe like your grandma's onion poultice."

"You know, I've been thinking," said Joe. "The way
you talked last night, I thought maybe you'd consider
letting me stay here with you this winter. Did you really
mean that? I'm a good worker, and I'd make myself
useful for my board. I'm a good hunter, too. But I don't
know whether you'd want me around."

"I guess we could use you," said Pop.

"Whoopee!" yelled Eggs.

Minty only smiled and heaped more pancakes on Joe's plate. It seemed suddenly as if all their troubles were over, if only Joe Boles would stay and help them through the winter.

· 8 ·

THE GRAND DUCHESS

"NOW THIS TEN-THOUSAND-DOLLAR PRIZE NOVEL CON-
test," said Pop, adjusting his spectacles and peering at
the contest magazine, "that's a little out of my class, I
believe. Ten thousand dollars is a lot of money, but then
it takes a terrible long time to write a novel, and I
never was one to sit down and write for a long spell.
This short-short story contest suits me better. The prize
is only a hundred dollars, but the writing is within
reason and oughtn't to give me writer's cramp."

Joe had come in with an armful of wood, which he
dropped noisily into the woodbox.

"Contests!" he snorted. "There's nothing in them.
They're all out to gyp you in one way or another."

"Joe, you come here a minute," said Pop. "Sit down
there on the other side of the table and take this pen
and ink and a piece of paper, and get busy."

"Say! you aren't going to get *me* to write any short-short stories, Mr. Sparkes. No, sir!" protested Joe.

"No, I'll do all the story writing that's to be done around here," said Pop. "But there's something else I want you to do, Joe. It's the only favor I'm going to ask of you all winter."

"What's that?" asked Joe, his curiosity aroused.

"I'm going to ask you to write a letter to your mother, Joe. No, you needn't throw down the pen like that. Just let me tell you what I have in mind."

"You're trying to double-cross me," said Joe angrily.

> *"But curb thou the high spirit in thy breast,*
> *For gentle ways are best, and keep aloof*
> *From sharp contentions,"*

said Pop. "That's what the poet Bryant says. Now, Joe, your poor mother will be nearly crazy worrying about you. I'm not asking you to go back to her yet, but you write her a letter and tell her you are safe and have a good place to spend the winter with a family to look after you. Tell her you'll write her again in the spring and ask her not to try to find you until then, because you want to have some time to think and plan your life."

Joe stood at the table, idly fingering the pen, his head lowered so that they could not see his face. The red flush of anger slowly receded. At last he said doggedly:

"If they get a letter, they'll find out where I am and come after me."

"I don't believe they will, Joe—not if you ask them not to. You needn't put any address on the letter, and if they read the postmark—why, Scandian Corners is a small town in a lot of wild country. They wouldn't be likely to find you out here, wintering in a summer cottage."

"I guess your mother would miss you a lot," said Eggs. Now that Joe was here to stay, she spent most of her waking hours at his elbow admiring everything that he did. She was there now, and looking up into his troubled face, she added: "*We* haven't even got a mother to write to."

"I guess you've got a good pop, though," said Joe hurriedly. He drew a chair out noisily and sat down at the table. For a moment he was silent, his brow furrowed in thought; then he pulled the paper toward him, dipped the pen in ink, and began to write with the same deliberate care which he used in carving bits of wood.

Dear Mother: Don't worry about me. I am in a safe place, staying with a family for the winter. Please don't try to find me. I will write you in the spring.

Love,
Joe

When he had finished, Joe pushed the letter over to Pop to read. Pop adjusted his spectacles and read it slowly; then he took the pen and wrote on the bottom of the sheet:

Joe is well and happy here. We like him. He's pretty nearly a man now, and needs a little time to think things out for himself. He won't forget you.

Your friend,
Pop

"That's a good job done," said Minty, smiling at them both, and Eggs let out one of her famous "Whoopee!"s.

Joe said nothing, but his face was somehow relieved and happy-looking as he sealed up his letter, and presently he began to whistle softly to himself.

"Now," said Pop in a matter-of-fact voice, "to get back to this short-short story of mine."

"What are you going to write about?" asked Minty.

"Well, I've been turning over in my mind a plot about a duchess, Minty."

"Did you ever know a duchess?" asked Minty in surprise.

"No, Minty, I never did, but I like to think they exist."

"They seem sort of unreal somehow," said Minty. "Couldn't you write about folks like us?"

"Who'd want to read about folks like us?"

"Well, it's kind of exciting living like this in somebody else's house, and Joe being broadcast over the radio and all," said Minty doubtfully. She had really thought that it was for a minute, but now it seemed less so. "Anyway," she went on hopefully, "you might write about a girl like Marcia."

"What could I write about her?"

"Oh, she lives in a summer cottage in the summer, and a winter house in the winter, and she goes to school and has plenty of clothes and books and everything she wants—"

"There's no story in that, Minty! It takes more'n that to make fiction. I'll stick to my duchess."

"Maybe so," said Minty with a sigh, but she could not help thinking that a girl like Marcia was more interesting than any duchess.

"Who is this Marcia you're always talking about?"

"Haven't you seen her?" asked the girls.

"I haven't seen any girl but you two since I came."

"Well, look here," cried Minty, propelling Joe into his bedroom. "She's here, right over your bed."

"You mean that snapshot?"

"Yes! Yes!" cried Eggs and Minty together, and, both talking at once, they began to describe Marcia Vincent in all her glory, as she had come to exist in their minds.

"You've done pretty well to make such a beauty queen out of a blurry snapshot, an old smock, and the address on an envelope," said Joe, a little scornfully. "She's probably an awful snob."

"Oh, no! not *Marcia!*" cried Minty.

"Look how pretty she is," begged Eggs, pointing to the photograph.

"I see she's got a nose and a mouth and the usual number of eyes," said Joe. "But girls don't interest me."

Eggs and Minty looked after him wistfully as he stalked out and, swinging the ax over his shoulder, went back to his woodpile.

"Do you think he meant that?" asked Eggs solemnly.

"Well, I knew he didn't think much of *us*," said Minty. "But you'd think that *anyone* would be interested in Marcia!"

Joe chopped wood and fished; Minty cooked and swept up. Eggs washed dishes and set the table, but all Pop did was to work on his short-short story.

"I'm glad he's got something to take up his mind while he's getting well," thought Minty. "It's a wonder he hasn't busted out and gone fishing."

"The name of my story," announced Pop the next evening, "is 'Tatiana's Secret or How the Grand Duchess Saved Her Pearls.'"

"Gee, Pop!" Eggs shouted, "yesterday she was only a duchess and today she's a grand one! How come?"

"There's no use being stingy with her!" defended Pop.

"That's an awful long title for a short-short story," said Joe.

"Well, they don't put any limit on the number of words in the title so far as I can see," said Pop. "I want to give 'em their money's worth."

"How shall we spend the hundred dollars when Pop wins the prize?" asked Eggs.

"We'll buy a new car," said Pop.

"No, you don't," said Minty suddenly, "not until you've paid the rent to Marcia Vincent, you don't."

"Even supposing you won the prize," objected Joe, "you can't get any kind of a car for a hundred dollars."

Pop sat down in the nearest chair with a discouraged flop. "You're all against me," he said plaintively. They looked at him and their practical young faces suddenly softened.

"Oh, no, we aren't!" cried Eggs, flinging herself into his lap and putting her arms about his neck.

"No, we aren't, Pop!" Minty put her arms about him from behind and kissed his bald spot.

"We're all on your side, Mr. Sparkes," cried Joe, holding out his hand. Pop began to smile again.

"Hey, girls! you're tickling me! Let go a minute and let me breathe. Hey, quit it! Quit it!" Everybody came out of the huddle pleased and laughing, and Minty ran for the pen and ink.

"I'll copy the story right out for you, Pop, in my best handwriting, and we'll send it in before the contest closes."

"I know what *I'll* do," said Eggs, "*I'll* enter the perfume company contest and win a pony. Then we'll just hitch him to the trailer, and we won't need any car."

"Now that's an idea, Eglantine!" said Pop.

"I'll call the pony Merrylegs."

"His legs will be sad if he has to pull all of you and the rest of the groceries!" Joe observed.

"We'll have the groceries inside us by spring," shouted Eggs.

"Look!" Minty exclaimed. "What's happening to the lamp? It's sort of fading away, like."

Everybody looked, and it was quite true that the light was growing dimmer every moment.

"It looks to me as if it needed filling," said Pop. "There are a couple of kerosene cans on the back porch."

Minty ran to the back porch.

"One's empty," she reported. She returned with the other one, shaking it to listen to the swish of kerosene. "And this one's nearly empty!"

"That's bad," said Pop. "Abe Lincoln read by fire-light in the long winter evenings, but it's kind of hard on the eyes in this day and age."

"Didn't we have any kerosene in the trailer?"

"No, sir. That's one thing we overlooked."

"We can't go all winter without a light!"

"I expect they keep kerosene in the grocery store at Scandian Corners," said Pop.

"I could walk into town and get it for you," said Joe, "but I'm not going into any grocery store! No, sirree! They were broadcasting for me over the radio in the last grocery store I went into."

Minty thought that the radio and nearly everyone else would have forgotten about Joe by now, but she did not like to say so. Joe was as proud of his publicity as an opera star, and it seemed a shame to spoil his pleasure by minimizing the danger that he might be discovered.

"I think *I* could make it," said Pop. But the other three were quite definite on that point. Pop was still too weak from his illness for the long walk to town.

Minty considered for a moment.

"I know the best way to do," she said. "I'm sure I can walk to town if I don't have to carry the cans. We'll go in together, Joe, and you can wait just outside town while I buy the kerosene, and then you can carry it home for me."

"All right," said Joe. "That ought to work."

"And you can mail Joe's letter and all of our contest entries," said Pop.

"How about taking me?" yelled Eggs.

"You must keep house for Pop. We'd have to carry *you* as well as the kerosene, if you went along," said Minty.

"Will you bring me something then?"

"Yes," said Minty. "I'll bring you something if you're good." She sighed a little as she went on copying Pop's story. There were so many things to do every day, and some of them were hard to manage.

· 9 ·

SCANDIAN CORNERS

THE NEXT MORNING MINTY AND JOE MADE AN EARLY start. Minty put some cheese between biscuits for their luncheon, and Joe strapped the empty kerosene tins in his packsack and fastened it to his back. Pop doled out a little money and advised them to get both cans full if they could carry them, as they had a long winter ahead. He was in fine spirits this morning, and as they set out they heard him reciting in a wistful voice:

> *"There is something in October*
> *sets the gypsy blood astir;*
> *We must rise and follow her."*

"Where does your pop get all those things he recites?" asked Joe as they swung along over the hill.

"Those are poems," said Minty. "They just rattle

around in his head. He's got a wonderful head for poems, but it's not so good for figures, it seems like."

"I never knew anybody like him," said Joe, "but I think he's fine."

"So do I!"

Seven miles is not a difficult walk on a bright autumn day. As Minty said, you had to keep moving to keep warm, and by noon they saw the small cluster of houses that made up the town of Scandian Corners. A little river wandered in a half loop about the edge of town. Beside the bridge stood a ruined sawmill, the last relic of the old lumbering business, and there was a big red icehouse which suggested the new business of the town —the summer tourists.

Joe and Minty found a sheltered nook among trees and bushes and ate the lunch they had brought. It tasted good after the long, cold hike, and they carefully divided the last biscuit and all the crumbs. Then Minty crossed the bridge and entered the town alone. After Chicago, Scandian Corners looked like some practical joker's idea of a town. There was one main street with several small residential streets straggling away from it into the country. There was a square cement-block bank, which looked to be the most solid and prosperous building in town, and surrounding it, like chicks about a hen, were a drugstore, two grocery stores, a café, a barbershop, a saloon, a shoemaker's shop, a blacksmith's shop, and a hardware and general store. Minty saw that there was a garage, too, behind the gas station. She hesitated for a moment, thinking, "I might go in and

see how much they'd charge to come and get our car. Maybe Pete Gustafson was wrong about the price." But, as she stood hesitating, another thought was much more insistent.

"We're all set for the winter. We're comfortable. We don't want to go on to Aunt Amy's. Better not inquire about the car until spring. *You don't mind if we stay, do you, Marcia?*" In her own thoughts Minty often talked to Marcia, and it seemed to her now that Marcia would have wanted them to stay.

The grocery store was warm and had a not-unpleasant smell of onions, coffee, new overalls, and kerosene. There was a candy counter, and a wire basket full of oranges which made Minty's mouth water. The cold sliced ham and bologna sausage looked appetizing, too. But Minty's natural good sense had had much discipline. Neither Eggs nor Pop could have got by the chocolate bars and sausage without spending their money, but Minty went straight to the main counter and bought her kerosene. When her cans were filled she had just five cents left, and she remembered that she had promised Eggs a present. She went to the glass candy case and looked in. Candy bananas, long strips of licorice, chocolate bars, peanut bars, peppermint sticks, and chocolate mice—everything looked so good! And then there were lollypops at a penny apiece!

"I'll take five lollypops, please," said Minty and she thought to herself, "that will be one for each of us with an extra one for Eggs."

She stuck the little striped bag of lollypops into her coat pocket, and, picking up a can in each hand, she started to stagger to the door.

When filled, the two cans were about all she could manage.

"Quite a load you got, sister," said a man who was sitting behind the stove. Minty noticed him for the first time. He sat tilted back with his coat flung open to the warmth of the stove, and on his vest there was a shiny metal star. Minty went cold all over. She knew a sheriff when she saw one!

"Yes, sir, I got quite a load," she said. She balanced

the cans for a moment on the edge of a barrel of potatoes and looked at him with wide eyes.

"Where do *you* live?" asked the sheriff kindly. "I never see *your* face before."

"It is sort of uncommon," said Minty evasively. She tried to smile.

"Your father got his wagon out there? You can't carry them things very far."

"I'm pretty strong," said Minty. "I guess it comes from lifting pigs." It was the first thing that came into her head. The sheriff laughed.

"Farm kid, eh?" he said. "Have you seen any runaway boys out your way? There's one wanted in the Twin Cities. Has he been around your place?"

"We don't see many folks out to our place," said Minty in a small voice. Joe had been right. They had not forgotten about him. The kerosene was slopping onto her hands. She hated the oily feel and the smell of it.

"Tell your old man you're too little to carry all them cans. He'd ought to come in himself," said the sheriff good-naturedly.

"I'll tell him," said Minty, struggling with the heavy door. At last she was out in the cold air again and hurrying to the river. When she finally reached the other side of the bridge, she was trembling like a leaf; and yet the sheriff had been all lazy kindness. As far as he was concerned, he had only been passing the time of day with a farmer's daughter. She knew that it was her own conscience which made her tremble.

Joe had been watching for her, and now he came out of the bushes and took the two cans and fell into step beside her.

"It was cheap of me to let you go into town alone," he said. "But I don't want them to find me now. Maybe I'll go back in the spring like your pop says, but I've got to have the winter to think it over. You believe that that's all right, don't you, Minty?" He looked at her earnestly as if he really valued her opinion.

"Yes, Joe," she said slowly. "I think you ought to take your own time. But it's a good thing you didn't come into town. They're looking for a runaway boy." She told him about the sheriff.

The seven miles seemed much longer going back than they had been coming. Minty's whole body ached with the walking and helping Joe carry the cans. Her old worn shoes had blistered her heels. Joe had an easy woodsman's stride, but the cans were heavy even for him, and they often stopped to rest. Occasionally a car or a farm wagon came along the road, but, instead of begging a ride, they usually stepped into the woods or behind a fence while it went by.

"Why don't you catch a ride if you can, Minty?" said Joe. "And I'll come along with the kerosene." Minty thought a moment. Then she said, "No, I'll stick along with you, Joe. It isn't so far now."

Before they reached the Gustafsons' farm and the little cross road that ran to the Vincent place, they saw the sun go down. It disappeared as they sat to rest on a knoll by the roadside. A great bonfire of crimson light flamed up the sky after the sun was gone. The earth looked strangely dark and green. The wind had fallen with the sun and not a dry leaf rustled or spun. Far away on the quiet air there was a rhythmic, throbbing sound, like the beating of some giant pulse. Faint and far it was, but with an urgent rhythm that somehow stirred the blood. They both listened and Minty turned her head and looked inquiringly at Joe.

"Tom-toms," said Joe softly, the listening look still in his face. "There's an Indian reservation a few miles over there. I skirted the edge of it the day I met you in the woods."

"Oh," said Minty. She had seen an Indian once at the Chicago Exposition.

By the time they reached the cottage it was dark with the early darkness of late autumn. But, tired as she was, Minty looked with wonder at the stars. They were not city stars, these glittering gems that blazed in the sky so thickly. They twinkled and glittered with a remote and icy splendor, and underfoot the dried grass and leaves rustled with frost.

Buster ran barking to meet them, and Eggs threw open the door of the cottage with a shout. How warm and light and pleasant it was inside!

"Home!" thought Minty. "We've come home!" There was a delicious smell of frying pancakes and bubbling brown sugar syrup and sizzling bacon.

"Name your poison, ladies and gentlemen," called Pop gaily. "Gollwhollicker? Sockdollager? Or whale?" He had a checked gingham apron tied about his waist and his spectacles were balanced precariously on the end of his nose.

"Whales!" cried Joe, and Minty added, "We're hungry enough to eat an uncooked cow!"

"Sorry," said Pop, "but ours come cooked."

· 10 ·

INDIAN VILLAGE

THE NEXT WEEKS WERE FULL OF OUTDOOR EXERCISE.
"Before snow flies we've got to do some heavy work
around this place," Joe had declared. Pop, who still
sneezed and coughed too much for heavy outside work,
took over the housekeeping, and Minty and Eggs were
Joe's helpers. Usually they took the boat and landed
at some wooded island or point across the lake, where
Joe went looking for wood. Joe was a good woodsman
and took only dead or fallen trees, improving rather
than spoiling the place he worked on.

"We've got to take care of our trees and woods," he
said. "My dad used to say that, every time we went out
hunting together. Nothing made him madder than to
see careless people slashing down live trees, or letting
forest fires get started. 'Don't you ever do that, Joe,'
he used to say."

The girls helped saw and chop, or made the small branches into bundles which they loaded into the boat. When the tree trunks were stripped of branches, they all worked to drag them to the lake, where Joe tied them together into a rough raft so that they could be towed home behind the boat. It was hard work, but it was fun. The woodpile grew higher and higher.

They took their lunch with them and ate it around a campfire on the beach. Joe took his gun, too, and often they brought home some partridges or a rabbit or a couple of squirrels for Pop to stew for their supper.

Buster loved to go with them, and, if they left him behind, he swam along after them looking so imploring that they usually ended by hauling him into the boat, wet shags, shakes, and all.

"He's the dumbest darn hunting dog I ever saw," complained Joe one day. "He just stirs up the woods and scares everything away."

"Don't you dare insult Buster," cried Eggs. "He learned to chase cats in Chicago, and you can't expect him to lie down and let the squirrels and rabbits run all around him just because he's in Wisconsin. How does he know they aren't cats?"

Joe laughed.

"Well, there's just one thing I hope he doesn't chase!"

"What's that?"

"It's a pretty little black animal with a bushy tail and a white stripe down its back."

"I guess you mean a chipmunk," said Eggs.

Sometimes through the still, cold air they heard the throb of Indian drums, and one day, when the wood was nearly all hauled in, the girls begged Joe to take them to the reservation.

"Is it awfully far to walk?" asked Eggs, who, although she ran and skipped for miles every day, hated the idea of a long straight walk to a given destination.

"It's pretty far," said Joe, "but I think there's an easier way to go."

Beside the front door in the living room the Vincents had pasted up a large map of the surrounding country with trails and water routes marked on it. Pop and the girls never bothered with maps, but Joe often studied it with his intense thoroughness. He went to it now and traced a route with his finger.

"If we took the canoe," he said, "we could go to the end of the lake, and portage across this short trail to the big lake beyond. Then, if we skirt around the shore there, we come to a channel that takes us into another tiny lake, and that's where the Indian village is. It would be shorter than to walk."

Pop adjusted his spectacles and looked over Joe's shoulder.

"All right," he said. "But you look out with that canoe. Canoes are awfully tricky things. They upset easy. I don't know whether you ought to go or not."

"Oh, please, Pop," begged the girls. There was nothing like a little opposition from Pop to make them crazy to do a thing.

"Well, take good care of yourselves, that's all I have to say," warned Pop, trying to look like a stern parent.

"It will take us the whole day, Minty," said Joe. "You'd better put up a good big lunch."

Joe's father had taught him how to handle a canoe, and for some time Joe had been teaching Minty to use the bow paddle. It was simply a matter of timing her stroke to Joe's and keeping it steady, for Joe did the steering from his place in the stern. They established Eggs and the lunch basket in the bottom of the canoe about the middle, and Pop shut Buster indoors, for decidedly Buster's excitable temperament was not wanted in a canoe. At the last moment Eggs decided to take a doll, which she had scarcely looked at for months.

"Good gracious!" protested Minty. "Whyever do you want to take that doll along? You don't care for her anyway, and you know you never play with her at home."

"She wants to see the world," said Eggs. "She won't make any noise or jump around in the boat, will you, Peacharino?" Peacharino was silent, even as Eggs had promised that she would be.

A wintry sun was shining and a stiff breeze helped them along. It seemed to Minty that the canoe shivered and leaped under it, as a spirited horse might do on setting out for a canter. When they reached the end of the lake, they pulled the canoe out of the water and looked about for the portage that Joe had seen on the map. The path from lake to lake was deep in leaves and looked as if it had not been used for a long time,

but there were still the old blazes cut on the trees, and
they soon picked it up. Joe got under the canoe near
the middle and lifted the main weight of it onto his
shoulders, and Minty took the lesser weight of the
stern. Eggs skipped along behind with a couple of
sweaters, the lunch, and her doll. She and the squirrels
chattered at each other as they passed. A quarter of a
mile brought them to the big lake, and there a cold
wind seemed to blow through them, and waves danced
threateningly.

"Keep your paddle in the water as much as possible,
and pull a long, steady stroke," said Joe. "It's rough
for a canoe, but we'll make it."

Minty shivered a little. How the wind howled and
shook the canoe! Up in the bow seat she seemed to be
almost on top of the waves, and they looked unpleasantly

active and cold. But she couldn't let Joe know that she
was afraid. If he said that they would make it, they
probably would, Minty thought hopefully. Eggs was
having the time of her life.

"Gee! this is fun!" she yelled. "It's just like a cradle
or a swing or something, being teetered around this
way! Peacharino is glad she came. It's awful cold,
though. What if we'd tip over in that water? I guess
that would be some surprise! Especially since Peacharino
and I can't swim. Do you see those big birds up there?
They're flying in a kind of point just like you see air-
planes do in the movies. What are those, Joe?"

"Wild geese," said Joe. His voice was calm and
steady in the wind. It gave Minty the feeling that
everything was all right. Her thin arms ached, but she
kept her stroke long and steady and her paddle in the
water.

"Hey!" shouted Eggs. "That last wave splashed right
in and hit me! I'm wet and I don't like that."

"Keep your seat," said Joe calmly. "She's rough
enough without any help from you, Eglantine."

"I'm kind of scared, Joe," said Eggs.

"About two minutes more and we'll be through the
worst of it."

Presently they were in the lee of the land and the
canoe felt steadier, like a spirited horse who has had his
run and is willing to settle into a quiet trot.

Minty drew her breath more easily again.

"Look at all those big houses along the bank," said
Eggs, forgetting her fright as soon as the worst was

over. "They're all closed up. They look like hotels. What are they for?"

"Summer resorts," said Joe. "Nobody's there now. It's winter."

"Gee! It sure feels like it!"

It was nearly noon before they found the passage for which Joe was looking. It was a narrow, winding channel through a marsh filled with swamp grass, cranberry, and wild rice. The rice and cranberries had all been harvested by the Indians, and only the brown grass waved and rippled in the wind.

"The Indians always harvest the wild rice," said Joe. "We better see if we can get some. It's good and it will help out a lot this winter."

"We didn't bring any money," said Minty.

"Well, maybe we've got something we can trade," said Joe.

When they had come through the channel, they saw a pretty sight. The last little lake was so sheltered that it was almost as quiet as a pond, and across the water from the channel was the reservation village. Bare and scant and poor it was, and yet it was somehow beautiful. It was built along a high bluff, and on one side rose the whitewashed spire of a mission church surmounted by a gold cross. At the other end of the village was a long, low building built of weathered boards and surrounded by evergreen trees which had been cut and stuck in the ground some time before and which were now dead and dried a rusty red. Between these two buildings straggled a number of weathered

log cabins and dilapidated clapboard houses, set irregu-
larly with no idea of order or alignment, and yet the
whole effect was picturesque and strange. It was as if
the meandering channel had led them into a foreign
land—a land that had nothing to do with Scandian
Corners or the summer resorts or the farm or tourist
people. The closer they came, the more desolate the
village looked. There was a small store, some fish nets
spread to dry on bushes, and a few birch-bark huts
built near the houses. The huts looked deserted now,
as if they were used only in summer. Faded clothing
flapped on clotheslines, and where a windowpane was
broken other faded garments were thrust in to keep
out the cold.

As the keel of the canoe grated on the beach, a dog
barked and several others joined him. Two small Indian
boys in overalls and ragged coats popped up from no-
where and helped drag the canoe on shore. Their flat,
brown faces were wreathed in smiles, but they said
nothing at all.

Before Joe, Minty, and Eggs had gone far through
the village, six more children had joined them in a kind
of solemn procession with three or four dogs brawling
and yelping behind.

"They don't still scalp, do they?" asked Eggs un-
easily.

"No," said Joe, laughing. "They're just curious."

It didn't take long to see the village, and Eggs was
clamoring for food.

"Let's ask them if we can eat our lunch in the store,"

suggested Minty. "I'm as cold as a fish and I'm tired of having all these little kids gawking at me."

"The wind's come up a lot just since we landed," said Joe. "It will be harder to cross the big lake going back than it was coming over." Minty shuddered.

"I don't think it could be worse," she said.

"Don't you fool yourself," said Joe. "But we've got to eat first anyway."

They pushed open the door of the store and found it full of smoke and men and a variety of smells, but at least it was warm. Minty pushed in too far for retreat and said, "May we eat our lunch here?" before she discovered that the central figure in the group of men was a white man whom she had seen before—the sheriff of Scandian Corners.

"Hello, sister," said he. "You get around right spry to do your shopping."

"Seems like you're in every store I go into," replied Minty.

"Has the kerosene supply run out?"

"Not yet, it hasn't. We just want a warm place to eat lunch."

"I guess Charley White Dog can find you a barrel to sit on, eh, Charley? You got a corner by the stove for these kids?"

Charley White Dog, the proprietor of the store, obliged with three apple boxes behind the stove. The men went on talking among themselves, and Minty maneuvered Joe into the darkest corner and Eggs next to him.

"Gee! who's your friend, Minty?" asked Eggs. "He's awful nice, isn't he?"

"Hush up!" hissed Minty. "You let me do all the talking, and I'll tell you later."

"But I'd rather know now," said Eggs.

"You do as I say!" said Minty. She handed Eggs a sandwich with a sweet, sisterly smile, but at the same time she trod on her toe to let her know that she meant business. Eggs joined Peacharino in awed silence. Joe was silent too, his cap pulled low on his forehead. The sullen look which he had worn the first day Minty saw him had returned to his eyes. Alert for danger signals, Minty listened as she ate, her ears and eyes wide open.

An old Indian seemed to be pleading with the sheriff for leniency toward his son. The son, a young man in his early twenties, stood by with hanging head.

"He very good boy," the old man kept repeating in a quavering voice.

"No, Henry," said the sheriff firmly. "I've got to take him. I've told you a dozen times what he done. He got drunk and broke into Mr. Larson's house and went to bed in Larson's bed."

"He not steal," said the old man.

"No, he didn't take anything, that's true. But it's pretty near as bad to enter another person's house without asking leave. He got mud on Mrs. Larson's sheets and he ate a cake she had setting on her sideboard. A person hasn't got any right to go in and use another person's house without permission. It'll do him good to cool his heels in jail for a week."

Minty couldn't help speaking. "Is that all he did, just stay overnight in somebody else's house?"

"Sure," said the sheriff, smiling at her. "Ain't that enough?" He clamped a handcuff on the wrist of the unprotesting Indian and fastened it to his own wrist. Then with his friendly smile he came and stood over Minty. Minty was sorry that she had made him notice her again.

"How did you kids get over here anyway?" he asked.

"We came in a canoe," said Minty.

"Canoe, eh?" said the sheriff. "Did you come through the big lake?"

"Yes."

"You'll never get back that way today, sister. She's sure boiling this afternoon and there's a worse storm coming. You could do it in a rowboat maybe, but, unless you're good swimmers, you better not try it in a canoe."

"I guess we'll make out," said Minty doubtfully.

"Look here, you kids, I'd hate to have to drag that big lake for you tomorrow. I've got room in the back of my car. You pile in there and I'll take you right to your own door. One of these Indian kids can bring the canoe across to your folks when the storm is over. How's that?" Minty was seized with panic. Right to their own door—the door of the Vincents' cottage! She could almost feel the cold steel of the handcuff on her wrist. She heard herself saying in a small, firm voice:

"That's mighty kind of you, Mr. Sheriff, but we aim to spend the night here."

"Well, that's all right then. But look out for your-selves. Are the other kids deaf and dumb?"

"No-o," gasped Minty, "just sort of speechless."

Joe made a sound that was something between a gasp and a grunt, and suddenly Eggs said in a clear voice:

"*Cuckoo, jug-jug, pu-we, to-witta-woo!*"

· 11 ·

HEATHEN DANCERS

WHEN THE SHERIFF WAS GONE, THEY BOLTED THE REST of their lunch and went outside. It was true that the morning's wind, which had seemed so strong, was now rapidly turning into a gale, and the little landlocked bay below the Indian village was being whipped into foam and thunder. What would the big lake beyond the channel be by now? But Joe was determined to go out and see. Before they were halfway through the channel, however, they could hear the crash of waves, and even Joe was willing to admit that the crossing was impossible when he saw the size of the waves on the big lake. Reluctantly they turned back to the Indian village.

"I didn't like the way that man talked about dragging the lake for us," said Eggs. "Did he mean we'd drown?"

"Well, it seems likely," said Minty.

"How far is it to walk home?"

"About ten miles by land, I guess," said Joe.

"Oh, gee!" cried Eggs. "I'd rather sleep here. You told the sheriff you were going to stay here, Minty."

"I know," said Minty gloomily. "I couldn't think of anything else, and I was scared to have him drive us home. He might have put handcuffs on all of us for living in the Vincents' cottage."

"I'd just roll up by a campfire and sleep outside if I were alone," said Joe, "but I'm afraid you girls would freeze."

"And we ate all of our lunch!" wailed Eggs.

"I'm thinking about Pop," said Minty. "He'll be scared stiff if we don't come home tonight. But I guess it would be better to get home tomorrow than not at all."

"I wish we hadn't ever come," said Eggs, dropping the corners of her mouth in preparation for a good cry.

They were standing on the beach now below the Indian village and the usual group of curious youngsters had gathered to greet them. The wind whipped their clothes about them and flapped their hair in their faces. One of the little girls had moved close to Eggs and was shyly fingering the dress of Eggs's doll, which hung limp and forgotten over her arm.

"What shall we do?" asked Minty, looking to Joe's superior wisdom.

"We'd never make it home tonight walking with Eggs," said Joe slowly. "We had better see if they can

put us up somewhere here." He looked as if the idea
were distasteful to him, and Eggs burst into tears.

"I'm scared," she announced.

"You want place to stay?" asked one of the young
Indians. "Come along, I show."

He led them briskly up the path to the village and
along the road to the whitewashed church. The road
bent sharply around a cluster of buildings which took
shelter behind the church. Everything here was spot-

lessly neat in contrast to the general untidiness of the
village. The Indian boy opened a gate in a whitewashed
picket fence, and they found themselves in a little garden, sheltered on three sides by the church and the low
white buildings. The sand paths were carefully swept
and marked off with white stones. The leaves had been
well raked beneath the bare fruit trees, and the garden
put in order for the winter. A very old man in a long
black cloak was carefully pruning away the super-
fluous branches on a young apple tree. He moved with
a slow grace as if time meant nothing to him. When
he saw them, he came forward to meet them, a smile
of welcome on his face.

The Indian boy spoke to him in the Indian language,
and the old man looked sharply at the three travelers
from under his shaggy white brows. But his smile was
kind.

"You want a place to stay, my children?" he asked.
Joe explained their predicament in a few words, and
Minty and Eggs nodded. They were rather awed by
the dignified appearance of the old priest. The little
Indians seemed in some awe of him, too, and even the
dogs lay quiet on the neat path, with tongues lolling
and eyes on his face.

"Yes, yes," he said gently when he had heard their
story. They told him everything except that they lived
in someone else's cottage and that the sheriff had offered them a ride home which they had been afraid
to take. "Yes, yes. It is very easily arranged. We have
more room here than we need nowadays. The boy shall
stay with me. What is your name, son?"

"Joe—Joe Boles." It came out in spite of himself.

The old priest smiled. "Joseph," he said. "That is a saint's name, my boy. Yes, he shall stay with me, and you must take the girls to Sister Agnes."

Looking very important the young Indians escorted Minty and Eggs to the side wing of the long, low building and rang a doorbell. Almost immediately, as if they had seen the little procession coming through the garden, the door was opened by two nuns.

Eggs was frightened again when she saw their long black veils and dresses, but the same sixth sense which had told Minty that she could trust Mrs. Gustafson told her now that she had found friends. Behind the strange black veils something warm and pleasant shone out of Sister Agnes' eyes. Her face was neither old nor young and quite plain-looking except for the eyes. The little Indians clustered around her, babbling and talking as if they loved her. Minty was surprised, after seeing them so solemn and unspeaking. The other nun, Minty thought, was beautiful and very young, too. Smiling, she hovered in the background, like a shy bird. Sister Catherine, they called her.

Minty had no need of explaining her errand, for the little Indians, now suddenly garrulous, had done it for her. Before she knew it, she and Eggs were taking off their things beside a stove in a plain, whitewashed room which contained rows of small desks and benches and had maps on the wall and plants in the windows.

"*School!*" said Eggs in consternation.

"Oh, yes!" said Sister Agnes with her low, musical laugh, "but it is all over for the day!"

Eggs gave a sigh of relief, and began to enjoy herself.

After the long day in the canoe and the wind and wandering about the village, the little mission school seemed very wonderful. Presently Sister Agnes showed them to a tiny room on the floor above. In it were two narrow white cots, a blue curtain behind which to hang their clothes, and a chest of drawers with a washbowl but no mirror. A crucifix hung on the wall and a little colored picture of a smiling saint. Around the white wall near the ceiling, someone had lettered the following text: FOR HIS EYES ARE UPON THE WAYS OF MAN AND HE SEETH ALL HIS GOINGS.

Sister Agnes lingered beside them a moment, her fluttering white hands smoothing the spreads, straightening the pitcher in the bowl, laying out two towels.

"Now you may wash," she said, "and there will be supper in half an hour."

"How did you know we were coming," asked Eggs, "so as to have everything all ready for us?"

"We are always ready for someone," said Sister Agnes, "but there are not so many who come to us now. Every year the number of Indians on the reservation grows smaller. Once our school was full, now it is almost empty." She sighed and the white hands rested for a moment on her breast like tired birds.

"We haven't any money to pay," said Minty. She always thought of that first, because so many times people were angry when they offered you something, and found that you could not pay for it. Sister Agnes looked at her with a kind of slow surprise. Then she smiled and her hands began to flutter again.

"God is your host, my dear," she said. "He wants only your love."

Supper was at a long table in a room below, and four Indian girls shared the meal with them. Two were orphan girls, and the homes of the others were too far away on the reservation to permit them to go back and forth to school every day. Sister Agnes sat at one end of the table and Sister Catherine at the other, and an Indian woman served them. Susie Whitefoot, they called her, and Minty thought that it might well have been Susie Lightfoot, because she moved so softly to and fro. Glancing down, Minty saw that the woman wore moccasins on her feet.

To Eggs and Minty the simple supper tasted delicious. There was meat and potato hash, fried a golden brown, with homemade biscuits and wild plum jam, and baked apples for dessert. As they were finishing the meal a low, insistent sound began to make itself heard in the room. One felt it almost more than heard it, a rhythmic beating of drums, now brought strongly to them on the wind, now dying away to a distant throbbing. Sister Agnes went on talking more brightly than ever, but the four Indian girls fell silent, their heads slightly turned, their eyes wide, as if they were listening, and one of them began to drum softly with her fingers on the table.

Just then there was a knock on the door, and, when it was opened, they saw Joe's face, glowing with wind and excitement, against the darkness of the garden. The beat and throb of the Indian drums blew in with the fresh night wind, and for an instant seemed to fill the room. Then Sister Agnes quickly drew Joe inside the room and closed the door as if to shut out the sound.

"The Indians are dancing," said Joe. "I want Eggs and Minty to come and see them." Eggs ran for her coat, but Minty hesitated. The sound of the drums had changed the simple atmosphere of this room into something tense and strange, and Minty did not understand it.

"May we go?" she asked slowly, looking at Sister Agnes. Sister Agnes and Sister Catherine exchanged troubled glances. Then Sister Agnes said, "They are the heathen Indians which you hear. Our Christian Indians do not dance." But she did not say, "You may not go," and Eggs was back with their coats, thrusting Minty's into her hands.

"We won't be long," said Joe. "I'll look out for them."

As they went out the door, Minty saw the Christian Indian girls still sitting at the table, their faces strained with listening to the heathen drums, and one of them still unconsciously tapped the heathen rhythm on the tablecloth.

Leaning into the wind, Minty, Joe, and Eggs hurried through the garden and up toward the village. Other dark figures were hurrying in the same direction, and now the drums were like excited voices calling, insisting, telling people to drop what they were doing and come. At the other end of the village was the long, low building which they had seen from the lake earlier in the day. Now it was lighted with smoky lamps, and, besides the sound of drums which issued from it, came the wailing song of voices, and the sound of shuffling feet, like rustling leaves.

Eggs clung to Joe's arm on one side and Minty's hand on the other. It was all strange, yet none of them wanted to turn back. The Indians made way for them at the door of the building, and presently they found themselves sitting on a narrow bench which ran all the way around the room. Withered fir branches decorated the walls and a rusty stove at the far end of the room sent out a hot glow. In the center of the floor on low boxes sat the four drummers whose savage rhythms set the pace for the dancers. The drums were crudely made kettledrums with skin stretched tight across the top, and, as the drummers played, they also sang—a high, nasal song in a minor key. Two of the drummers were young, two old, and Minty saw that one of these was the old man whose son had been taken by the sheriff.

Indians old and young crowded the floor to dance. Most of them wore white men's clothing in various degrees of shabbiness. But some had come dressed for the occasion in beaded vests or skirts or jackets trimmed with dyed porcupine quills and bits of shining looking glass. Some of the older men wore feathers in their hair and some wore circles and queues of feathers fastened to their backs like switching tails.

Many of the children whom they had seen during

the day were here dancing, although Minty was sure that they were pupils of Sister Agnes at the mission school. Indeed it seemed to be a not entirely un-Christian gathering, for here and there among the gaudy beads was the gleam of a cross on the neck of some forgetful dancer.

At first only the men and boys were dancing, twisting themselves about in fantastic motions and switching the feather tails. The women laughed and nodded, sometimes softly clapping their hands in the rhythm of the drums. Then there was a pause and the rhythm changed. Now the women and girls came out, giggling and ducking their heads, and shoving each other forward, and presently they were shuffling about in a big circle

with an awkward little side step. A thin old woman,
with no teeth and a face like a withered apple, led the
dance, her eyes bright and her step as sprightly as any
girl's.

The little girl who had admired Eggs's doll in the
afternoon came up now and shyly took Eggs's hand.

"Want to dance?" she asked. Eggs needed no second
invitation. In a moment she and the Indian girl had
fallen in behind the old toothless squaw and were
shuffling sidewise with the best of them.

"Oh, me!" said Minty. "If Aunt Amy could see
her now!"

Joe laughed. "Leave her alone," he said. "She's having a beautiful time."

Cinderella at the ball could not have been happier
than Eggs. She danced the whole evening. Even when
the Indian women and girls sat sedately on the benches,
Eggs pranced and cavorted behind the little boys, to
the amused delight of the Indians. There was only one
dance that Eggs couldn't master, and that was the
feather dance. Only a few of the most agile young
braves attempted that. A feather was placed on the
floor, and the young men, their hands clasped behind
them, danced around it, each time they came near it
bending lower and lower until one finally succeeded
in picking the feather up with his lips.

The room grew stifling hot and close with so many
dancers, and Minty felt her head whirl with the long
fatigue of the day. At last Joe looked at his watch.

"Ten o'clock," he said. "This may go on all night.

We better go or we'll be locked out of the mission."
It was a difficult matter persuading Eggs, but finally
they got her out into the cold night air.

"Oh, gee!" she said regretfully. "I wish I was an
Indian!"

Sister Agnes was waiting up for them. She lighted
a candle and led them up the stairway and the dark
hall to their room. The mission seemed very cold
and quiet now after the heat and noise and confusion of
the dancing place. Sister Agnes' long black skirts whispered in the silent hall, and the candlelight made her
shadow large and strange upon the wall.

"You—enjoyed the dancing?" she asked politely. Eggs
nodded sleepily. She was too worn out to speak.

"It was very interesting," said Minty, "but sort of
queer and awfully hot."

"They are heathen," said Sister Agnes sadly, "but
God will forgive them."

When she was gone Minty helped Eggs to bed, and
slowly got ready herself. The candlelight flickered over
the text that was printed on the wall: FOR HIS EYES
ARE UPON THE WAYS OF MAN AND HE SEETH ALL HIS
GOINGS.

It had been an exciting day—one of the strangest
that Minty had ever known. The canoe trip, the Indians, the sheriff, Sister Agnes, and—God. Minty had
never thought much about God, but He seemed to be
as real a person here as the sheriff or Sister Agnes or
the old man who beat the drum. Sister Agnes had said
that God was their host, and God saw everything. He

saw the Sparkeses living in the Vincents' cottage and
Joe running away from home, and Eggs dancing with
the heathen.

Slowly Minty went down on her knees on the cold
floor.

"Oh, God," she said, "we aren't as bad as we look.
Please forgive us our sins, and thank you for being
our host. Amen."

· 12 ·

A VOICE ON THE RADIO

THE WIND WENT DOWN IN THE NIGHT, AND JOE CAME for them early in the morning to tell them to be ready to start back. Sister Agnes had asked the Indian woman to make them a luncheon of sandwiches and apples, and she stood in the mission door and watched them until they passed through the garden gate and disappeared. A crowd of Indians came down to the shore to see them off. The little girl who had been Eggs's dancing partner on the previous night brought them a birch-bark basket full of wild rice as a parting gift. Impulsively Eggs thrust Peacharino into her arms in return, and the two girls smiled and waved as long as they could see each other.

"I guess Pop will be proud of me," said Eggs, "bringing home something for us to eat this winter, and

Peacharino can go right on having adventures with the Indians. I don't think she'll miss me very much."

"It was nice of you, Eggs," said Minty. "That little girl had her eye on Peacharino from the moment we landed."

"Well, it doesn't look as if they have many toys, and they don't have any picture shows or things. I guess they just dance to give themselves a good time."

The lakes were calm now and the journey homeward uneventful.

As they drew nearer to the cottage, they kept wondering what Pop would be doing and thinking.

"I hope they haven't started to drag the lake for us," remarked Joe with a rueful laugh.

"Pop takes things pretty calmly," said Minty. "He'll think of something the poets said about not worrying, and he'll be all right."

Minty was quite correct. When they burst into the cottage that afternoon, they found Pop and Mrs. Gustafson calmly facing each other across the table and drinking coffee. Pop was saying,

"Hope, like the gleaming taper's light,
Adorns and cheers our way;
And still, as darker grows the night,
Emits a brighter ray.

"That's what the poet Goldsmith had to say about a worry like mine, Mrs. Gustafson."

"You don't say so!" ejaculated Mrs. Gustafson in admiration and astonishment. Then Eggs and Minty were

in Pop's arms and everything was being discussed and
explained and repeated again and again. Such an adven-
ture as they had had was worth many retellings.

Mrs. Gustafson shared their adventures for a little
while. Then she rose and said, "I got to be getting home.
Milking time is coming. I sure was surprised to find you
folks still here, but if you're renting from the Vincents
I guess it's all right. Only it's the first time I ever knew
them to rent the place. How much rent did they ask
you?"

"We figure to pay, er, fifteen dollars a month," said
Pop.

"Seems fair enough," said Mrs. Gustafson. "Sometime I write Mis' Vincent a letter and tell her everything is fine. You folks look like real nice people, but
it ain't always so. Last year a man and boy who robbed
a bank in Chicago hid out all winter in a cottage on this
lake. Nobody knew they was there until the spring
came. Then, when the sheriff went to get them, they
lit out and got away. You should have seen the mess
they left the cottage in."

"We aren't going to leave a mess here," Eggs said.
"We're real good housekeepers."

"And we're paying rent," said Minty.

"Sure, I know," Mrs. Gustafson said. "I wasn't talking about nice folks like you. But you can't trust no
strangers in these woods in winter. Right up here is
where the Chicago gangsters head whenever they get
in trouble in the city. They're mean men, them
gangsters."

The girls looked at Joe and grinned. He was standing behind Mrs. Gustafson, and now he put on a mock scowl and made his fingers into guns.

"Stick 'em up, podner," he said in a soft voice. "Ack-ack-ack-ack-ack!"

"What you say?" asked Mrs. Gustafson, turning around politely.

"Nothing, ma'am," said Joe with a shamefaced grin. The girls had a hard time keeping their faces straight.

"Well, like I tell my kids," said Mrs. Gustafson, "don't never open your door to strangers in winter. You never know who you find."

"We'll remember that, Mrs. Gustafson," said Pop, "and thanks again for the milk and eggs. You're a very kindhearted lady."

"We got more than we need now the summer folks is gone—butter, too. Come get them when you need them. And I sure am glad your kids got home safe, Mr. Sparkes."

"Believe me, I am too," said Pop.

After Mrs. Gustafson had gone, Minty said soberly, "Do you think she'll really write to the Vincents about us?"

"Maybe she will," said Pop calmly, "but I'm willing to bet against it. Mrs. Gustafson is a fine woman and I admire her, but I believe she'd rather milk fifty cows and bake a hundred loaves of bread than sit down and wrestle with one letter."

"Why did she come here?" asked Joe.

"She came to bring me my mail," said Pop importantly.

"Bless my soul! Where did I put it? I think it's an answer to one of my contest entries."

"Here it is, Pop, and here are your spectacles," cried Eggs.

"Suppose our fortune's made?" asked Pop, looking around at them all, over the tops of the spectacles, as he slit open the envelope. They looked back with wide eyes and parted lips. For the moment even Joe had nothing scornful to say about contests. It seemed an eternity that Pop was slitting open the envelope and pulling out the contents, and then they all saw that what he held in his hands was not a check for a hundred dollars, but Minty's carefully written copy of "Tatiana's Secret or How the Grand Duchess Saved Her Pearls." Out of its folds fluttered a little printed slip.

Minty picked it up and read, "Manuscripts not considered unless typewritten."

There was a long moment of silence. Then Pop gave a brief sigh and said, "But perhaps—if it had been typewritten—" and there was a small grain of comfort in that.

Snow came a few days later, driving in from the lake in gusts and flurries and coating the lakeward side of trees and branches with thick white. With the first flurries of snow came a flurry of letters for Pop and Eggs from the various contests that they had entered. The perfume company, which had offered the pony, wanted Eggs to purchase five dollars' worth of perfumery to sell to her friends and neighbors before she was eligible for another contest in which the winner would receive the pony.

"But I haven't got five dollars or any friends and neighbors!" wailed Eggs.

The sponsors of the limerick contest, which Pop had entered, wrote that unless he subscribed to their magazine his limerick would be disqualified. There was a catch in everything, for each contest Pop had entered seemed more anxious to sell him something than to give him a prize.

Minty and Joe took the disappointments calmly enough, because they had never put great faith in Pop's ability to win contests; but to Pop and Eggs this failure was little short of tragedy. They had been so sure that fame and fortune were just around the corner, and now with every letter the beautiful mirage of air castles moved further away and seemed more unattainable.

At last in December came Pop's first glimmer of good luck. The Spring Field Butter Company sent him a dollar bill for winning one hundred and fifth place in the poetry contest. Pop had borne the rest of his disappointments with fortitude, but now he was mad.

"One dollar for Gray's 'Elegy in a Country Churchyard'!" shouted Pop. "It's monstrous, that's what it is! It's an insult to the muse of poetry!"

"Now, Pop," soothed Minty, "you said yourself that the Spring Field Butter part of the poem was your own. There were only about three lines of Gray's 'Elegy'."

"Nevertheless," said Pop with dignity, "it's monstrous. I don't care so much for Charley Sparkes, but it breaks my heart for Thomas Gray."

"A dollar is better than nothing," said Joe.

"It will pay part of the postage you have spent."

"Shucks!" said Pop. "I'm through now! I've entered my last contest, kids, do you hear?"

"Yes, Pop, but how are we going to pay the rent and get our car fixed?"

"I don't know," said Pop gloomily. "I only know this, that the Sparkeses' honor won't allow me to soil my hands with another contest. My mind is made up."

Mrs. Gustafson's offer of milk had been gratefully received, and Minty often went after it. She loved the warm kitchen, full of blue-eyed children and the smell of fresh bread and coffee. There were times when she woke at night and trembled to think that the Gustafsons might have written to the Vincents about their summer cottage. It was only at night, when the wind howled and branches tapped the windows, that Minty remembered to worry. Her days were so packed with work and fun that worry was crowded out, and in the Gustafsons' kitchen all her fears were lost in the friendly welcome that she received. The Gustafsons were the last link connecting her with the outside world, and sometimes Minty sat a while to listen to the radio. For two months now the Sparkeses had been so shut away from newspapers and the noise and traffic of a big city that it seemed almost unbelievable, in this country kitchen, to hear news flashes from Chicago or music and advertising from Minneapolis. Cities went on as usual, but how far away they seemed until the radio brought them close.

"Weather forecast for tomorrow: much colder with

more snow for northern Wisconsin. . . . Police officers are asked to be on the lookout for two robbers who held up the teller of the Lake City Bank in North Chicago during the noon hour yesterday. They are said to be driving a stolen car and heading north. A reward is offered for information leading to their arrest."

"What I tell you?" asked Mrs. Gustafson. "They're probably heading north all right. The woods up here is full of them guys."

"Oh, gee!" Minty said.

But now there was another voice on the radio. The Silver Seal Flour commercial had begun.

"Attention, housewives," said a fluting feminine voice. "The Silver Seal Flour Company wishes to remind you that there are only six more days left before the end of their four-thousand-dollar recipe contest. The first prize of one thousand dollars will be awarded for the best breakfast recipe using Silver Seal Flour, and there are fifty additional prizes. Send in your favorite breakfast recipe and win one of these valuable prizes. Send it to Contest Department, Silver Seal Flour Company, Minneapolis, Minnesota . . ."

Minty took her bucket of milk and started back to the Vincent cottage. Yes, it was cold enough for more snow and the sky was heavy gray. But it was lovely, Minty thought. She liked the bare branches against the gray sky. At this season, when all the leaves had fallen, you could see the real shapes of the trees. Some sent their branches up in orderly rows, the twigs growing smaller and smaller as they reached for the sky. Other trees grew outward in a broad sweep of curving boughs, and some were a tangle of unplanned twigs and branches, like a maze or puzzle. The trees had begun to seem like people to Minty. This one was stern and remote, but the next one leaned down and smiled as you went by.

"Oh, I am happy here," Minty thought. As she walked along the deserted road other thoughts came to Minty. She seemed to hear again the fluting voice of the radio announcer. "Attention, housewives," it said. "The Silver Seal Flour Company wishes to remind you—" To remind you of what? Of a contest! Four thousand dollars in prizes for recipes! Only six days left!

Suddenly Minty began to run. One thousand dollars for a breakfast recipe using Silver Seal Flour. Pancakes, sockdollagers, gollwhollickers, *whales!* Here was a contest that Pop might stand some chance of winning.

Slip-slop went the Gustafson milk as Minty legged it for home.

· 13 ·

DETECTING
POP'S SECRET

"NO," SAID POP. "*The burnt child dreads the fire.* I TOLD you the other day that I was through with contests."

For the past half hour Minty and Eggs and even Joe had been trying to persuade Pop to enter Grandma Sparkes's pancake recipe in the Silver Seal Flour contest, but Pop just sat by the fire and rocked and smoked his pipe and shook his head.

"You were so crazy to enter contests a little while ago, Pop," cried Minty. "Please try just one more."

"Well, look what came of all my work, Minty. A measly dollar bill!"

"But you aren't very good at writing short-short stories and poetry, Pop, and you *can* make pancakes."

"No," said Pop, "I'm finally convinced. You and Joe tried mighty hard to tell me that contests were

the bunk, but I had to learn from experience. Now I
know you were right.

> *"I know that man*
> *May profit by his errors, and derive*
> *Experience from his folly,*

as the poet Shelley says."

"Oh, bother the poet Shelley!"

"Now, you be respectful to the poet Shelley, Eggs."

"Listen, Pop, how are we going to pay rent to the
Vincents if we can't make any money?"

"Well, if I thought we'd make any money on this

contest, I'd enter it, Minty. But contests are the bunk."

"Will you give us the recipe and let us enter it?"

Pop took his pipe out of his mouth and considered this request seriously.

"I like to be agreeable, Minty," he said, "but somehow I feel like this: that recipe is the only thing I've ever been real successful with. Now, if I enter it in a contest and it doesn't win the prize, I'm going to lose my self-respect. Don't you see? It's more than just a contest. It's the Sparkes honor that's at stake."

There was nothing more to be said after that. They all knew that Pop's self-respect needed all the bolstering it could get, and, if he felt that way about his pancakes, there was no use trying to persuade him. Still Minty couldn't get the idea out of her head. Four thousand dollars to be given away for breakfast recipes using flour, and the famous Sparkes gollwhollickers not even in the running! It seemed too bad.

"Don't you know how he makes 'em?" asked Joe later, when the three young people were alone.

"No, he won't tell me until I'm eighteen," said Minty. "It's Pop's one great secret."

"He uses flour and milk and eggs and butter," said Eggs.

"Yes, and salt and sugar and baking powder," said Minty, "but I don't know the quantities. That's what's important, and the way he mixes them in. They're not just ordinary cookbook pancakes."

"Let's all watch him," said Joe. "Maybe we could

find out how he does it, and you could send the recipe yourself."

"But there are only six days left in the contest," said Minty, "and besides he doesn't want us to."

"He'd be glad enough of the money if he won a prize, and, if he didn't, you needn't ever tell him," said Joe. Minty thought this over. The more she thought, the more certain she felt that this was the one contest in all the world that Pop stood any chance of winning. But, even supposing that she could spy out the secret recipe in the next six days, there still remained Pop's feeling about the Sparkes honor. She wondered what Marcia would do in her place—or what Sister Agnes would do. There used to be only Minty Sparkes to think about when there was a question of right or wrong to decide and the decision didn't much matter. Then Marcia Vincent had come, and now Sister Agnes, to stand behind her like good angels to be consulted on all important matters. She slipped into Joe's bedroom now to take a look at Marcia. It was too bad that the snapshot was so dim and blurry. Minty had to use her imagination to fill in what the picture lacked. There was a confident smile on the lips and about the shadowed eyes. "They must be blue eyes," Minty thought, "to go with the long blond hair."

The hair was so like the hair of a princess in a fairy tale. "Rapunzel! Rapunzel! Let down your long hair!"

"White and golden Lizzie stood
Like a lily in a flood."

One of Pop's poets had said it, but Minty couldn't remember which one. If you substituted *Marcia* for *Lizzie*,
it was a nice description of the girl in white with the
long braids.

Suddenly Minty was filled with resolution. This warm
house, this happy life in wild country, this secure and
independent winter—all were gifts from Marcia. If they
couldn't pay Marcia the rent, then there would be no
Sparkes honor to defend. Paying the rent was more
important than sparing Pop's feelings, and Minty knew
that she must do her best to get Pop's secret recipe. If
only there were more than six days left in which to
do it!

She took Eggs and Joe into her confidence, and they
decided that all their efforts would be needed if the
recipe was to be mailed in time. The first day it was
Eggs who asked Pop to make pancakes for supper, and
Pop declared with surprise that he had never had such
willing helpers. Minty and Eggs hovered about, antici-
pating his every need, fetching eggs, sugar, and flour,
and running for spoons and measuring cups.

"I'll measure the flour for you, Pop. How many cups?"

"Don't rattle me, girls. Just pass me the cup, and I'll
do the measuring myself."

"Will you be needing a teaspoon or a tablespoon for
measuring the baking powder?"

"Well, you might bring both, and I'll use my own
judgment."

"He's impossible," said Minty, when the three con-
spirators were alone in the kitchen after supper. But

they compared notes as they did the dishes, and it
turned out that they had fared better than they expected.
Joe had seen the size of the butter lump; Eggs could
tell how many eggs Pop had used, because she had
counted the number in the basket before and after Pop
had taken it; and Minty had obtained measurements of
the flour. But the measurements of baking powder, salt,
and sugar were small and hard to see, and Eggs declared that there was something else Pop had put in
which must have been nutmeg or cinnamon or some
kind of spice because it came out of a little box, which
Pop whisked back on the shelf so quickly that she could
not identify it afterward.

The next day it was Joe who asked for pancakes,
but it looked as if they weren't going to make much
progress, for Pop said:

"Here, you kids, clear out. You don't leave me room
to work my elbows. I don't mind making sockdollagers,
but I won't be joggled. *Space, and the twelve clean
winds of heaven*, that's what I want, as the poet says."

They retired from the kitchen with crestfallen looks.

"Do you think he suspects?"

"What shall we do?"

"It's no use asking him to make pancakes if we can't
look on!"

In the midst of this dismal discussion, a loud ki-yi-ing
broke out on the front doorstep.

"Something's happened to Buster," shrieked Eggs,
and, forgetting sockdollagers and gollwhollickers, they
all dashed for the front door. There sat Buster full of

shame and woe, lifting his voice toward heaven in queru-
lous complaint.

"Merciful goodness!" yelled Eggs. "He's got needles
in his nose."

"Needles nothing!" scoffed Joe. "He's gone and stuck
his schnozzle on a porcupine."

"Porcupine?" wailed Eggs. "What's that?"

"You know," said Minty, "it's that thing that the
poet Shakespeare and Pop are always talking about:

> "*Make each particular hair to stand on end*
> *Like quills upon the fretful porpentine.*"

"Oh, gee! Is that what fretful porpentines are good
for? Oh, my darling Buster!"

They brought Buster indoors and doctor Joe took
charge. Pop left his pancakes and came to help hold
Buster's legs and head, while Joe, with a pair of tweezers
from his father's kit, carefully removed the cruelly
barbed shafts from the dog's nose.

"Gee! Pop," remarked Eggs excitedly, "it looks as
if the poet Shakespeare wasn't all hot air after all!"

"It's about time that porcupine was going to sleep
for the winter," said Joe. "Buster must have scared up
the last one awake in the woods. Minty, do you want to
mix up some baking soda in a little water? That's good
for all kinds of stings and burns, and I guess it'll take
some of the pain out of Buster's nose."

Minty ran to obey. The baking soda stood on the
shelf beside the stove in the kitchen where the baking
powder and salt and other cooking things were kept,

and, as she reached for it, Minty couldn't help seeing that Pop had measured out a half teaspoonful of salt and left it beside the bowl of flour and a cup of milk, and that the box of nutmeg stood near by. There was a little sugar, too, poured over the flour, surely no more than a tablespoonful. She made rapid mental notes as she mixed Buster's poultice.

"Good old Buster!" she smiled to herself. "He's done more than any of us toward getting the recipe. Now all I need to know is how much baking powder, and, if I can't get that today, I'll try again tomorrow."

The next day, with a teaspoon in one hand and a can of baking powder in the other, Pop exclaimed:

"Say, you kids do have the biggest appetites I ever saw. You've eaten enough pancakes in the last three days to stock a hotel. It's a good thing we've got plenty of flour."

But Minty wasn't listening to Pop. She was busy scribbling something on a scrap of paper, for now she knew the whole recipe for the famous Sparkes pancakes. When she had finished writing, she caught up her coat and cap and ran out of the door on her way to the Gustafsons'.

"Say! What in tarnation is the matter with that girl?" exploded Pop. "I thought she was starving for pancakes, and just when they're ready to eat, out the door she goes like she'd sat on a bee!"

Joe and Eggs exchanged amused glances and Eggs clapped her hands noiselessly together several times to indicate her secret delight.

"I guess she's off her feed," said Joe. "A little air will do her good."

"I'll eat her share," offered Eggs.

Minty ran most of the way to the Gustafsons' with snow blowing in her face and wind plucking at her thin coat, but she was in time for the postman. She heard his car on the road and ran down to the gate to meet him.

"Lucky you got your letter in today, girl," he said, with a laugh. "If it keeps on snowing like this, I may not get through tomorrow, an' that's a fact."

He handed her the mail for the Gustafsons, and on her way back she stopped at the house to deliver it. As she handed in the letters, she saw that one of them had the name "Vincent" written in the upper left-hand corner. Her heart suddenly stood still and then began to pound. Why were the Vincents writing to the Gustafsons at this season of the year? Was it about their winter tenants?

"Come in, I make you some coffee." Mrs. Gustafson smiled, holding the door open against the blowing snow.

"No, thank you," said Minty wistfully. "You'll be reading your mail, and I—I'd better go home."

The snow spread white around her, and, when she had gone a little way, she found that the tracks she had made in coming over were already obliterated by the soft, blowing whiteness. She was wet to her knees when she reached the cottage, and she was glad to stand by the open fire while Pop fried the pancake batter that he had saved for her. Eggs helped her pull off her wet shoes.

"Well, of all the crazy girls!" said Pop. "You went all the way to the Gustafsons' and forgot to bring the milk! I wouldn't have been surprised to see myself do a thing like that, but you, Minty—!"

"Never mind," said Joe. "Minty's a real smart kid just the same."

· 14 ·

STRANGERS IN
A BLIZZARD

DARKNESS CAME EARLY THAT NIGHT. FOR HOURS THE
lake had been blotted out by a wall of whirling snow-
flakes, and gradually the white wall grew gray and came
nearer and nearer until the inside of the cottage seemed
the only warm, light haven left in the world. During
the day Joe kept a path open to the woodshed and the
lake, but soon even these faint, white trails were lost
in drifting snow.

"This is what I like," said Pop. "Plenty of wood to
keep warm, enough food to keep from starving, and a
cozy house shut off from the troubles of the world.
Come, gather around the fireplace, and I'll read you
what the poet Whittier says about being snowbound."

It was fun to be together here in the cottage. Tonight
they had just finished the supper dishes. Pop had filled

his pipe and taken a book of poems from the shelf. The
fire crackled pleasantly. The one lamp that they allowed
themselves threw its friendly beams out across the falling snow. Joe was carving a wooden rabbit tonight,
and Minty was stitching an old piece of canvas, which
she had found in the storeroom, into the lining of Eggs's
coat to make it warmer. Eggs was cutting paper dolls
out of a six-month-old fashion magazine. They were
secure and warm, and all the outside world seemed far
away.

"... *as zigzag wavering to and fro*
   Crossed and recrossed the winged snow," read Pop.

"*And ere the early bedtime came*
   The white drift piled the window-frame,
   And through the glass the clothes-line posts
   Looked in like tall and sheeted ghosts."

"Gee! That's just like us, isn't it?" said Eggs. "Only
I guess we haven't got any clothesline posts. But I'll
bet that those little evergreen trees outside look like
ghosts now, don't you?"

They all turned to the window to look, but what
they saw was so unexpected that Eggs let out a whoop
of terror, and the others started to their feet. Someone
had been looking in at them—a strange face, not Pete's,
nor Mrs. Gustafson's, nor even the sheriff's! A strange
face at the window! And they were seven miles from
town and deep in a blizzard.

"There's a man out there," shrieked Eggs. No one
else spoke for a moment. Then Pop said calmly:

"Well, keep your shirt on, Eglantine. The world is full of men of one sort and another."

"Not out here, it isn't," said Joe, pulling on his boots in a businesslike manner.

"He's probably lost his way in the storm," said Pop. "Put on the coffeepot, Minty, and you, Joe, bring him in. There's no use in him skulking around outside when he might as well enjoy a fire."

"Pop!" cried Minty. "Mrs. Gustafson said never to open up for strangers. Don't you remember?"

"That's just fine," Pop said. "But look what kind of a night this is. Anyone could die out there tonight in this storm. It might be us, Minty, if we didn't have this place to stay in. Let's not be selfish."

Pop's voice was matter-of-fact. Minty couldn't argue with him.

As Joe went out a cold blast of snow-laden air swept in and the lamp flickered and smoked. It seemed a long time that Joe was gone. The fire crackled on the hearth. Outside the wind whistled.

"Put on the coffeepot, Minty," repeated Pop.

Obediently Minty went to the kitchen, but her heart thumped heavily. It was frightening, when they all felt so secure, to look out of the window and see a strange face staring in.

Finally they heard a stamping of boots on the door-step, and felt another rush of air as Joe reopened the door.

"Two of 'em," he said laconically, and ushered in a tall man who carried a young boy in his arms.

"We saw your light," said the man hoarsely. "We lost our way. It's some storm!"

"So it is," said Pop. "Come right in. We weren't exactly expecting visitors, but make yourselves right at home. Everything we have is yours. Here, come up to the fire, sir. Is the youngster hurt?"

"I don't think so," said the man. "Just cold and exhausted. Couldn't go a step farther. Our car stalled in a drift down the road a little way."

"Well, fancy that!" said Pop. "Our car stalled on us, too. That's why we're here to greet you."

"We had a fight to get here, I can tell you. I thought

we'd never make it." He laid the boy gently on the couch, and then stood erect and shook himself like a dog. The wet snow fell about him in a shower.

Standing suspiciously in the kitchen doorway, Minty looked at the strangers. She saw that the man was dressed in rough, woodsman's clothes, and that he was tall and powerfully built. His face was dark and distinguished, and somehow at variance with the rough clothes he wore.

There was an odd look about the boy, too, something too fragile for the heavy boots, the patched breeches, and the old smudged leather jacket. His face looked blue and pinched in the lamplight. His hair was curly and dark and closely cropped over the ears.

"How come you got off the highway onto our little road?" asked Minty.

"There was a man we wanted to see in Scandian Corners. But he wasn't there and they sent us out to a farm on Birch Lake to find him. This road was the shortest way back to the highway. We were going to spend the night at the Gustafsons'."

"You know the Gustafsons?"

"The man we saw told us they'd take us in."

"Well, any friend of the Gustafsons is a friend of ours," said Pop hospitably. "Where's that coffee, Minty? This is no time to stop and stare."

In a moment they were forcing some coffee between the boy's colorless lips, and pulling off his mittens to chafe his hands. He gave a little fluttering gasp, and the color began to return to his cheeks. Suddenly he

sat up, looking wildly about him, as if the lights and
faces frightened him.

"It's all right, Topper," said the man. "We're out of
the storm."

"Oh, gee, Dad! I didn't think I'd pass out like this."

"Take it easy, take it easy! Everything's okay now."

"I feel as if I didn't have any feet."

"You've probably frosted them," said Joe. "You
mustn't heat them up too soon. I'll get you a pan of
cold water to soak them in."

"Let me help with your boots," cried Minty. Her
fear had begun to dissolve in a desire to help. Later they
could face their unknown problems, but at the moment
these people needed care. She knelt at the boy's feet and
began to unlace the heavy boots. They were caked with
snow and the laces frozen together. It was difficult to
get them off. But at last they were loosened and Minty
pulled them off one after another. Next came the heavy
gray socks, and Minty looked at the small, frosted feet.
They were narrow and white and nicely formed—a girl's
feet! This wasn't a boy after all. Startled, Minty looked
up at the face above her. A pair of startled dark eyes
looked back at her.

"You're a girl!" Minty said.

"Is that a crime?" For several seconds Minty and the
stranger looked at each other. Hostility and suspicion
were in their faces. Pop was busy talking with the man,
Joe was getting a pan of snow water, Eggs had run
for a towel. Minty was all alone with the strange girl
and her secret.

"What are you doing way out here on a night like this?" she asked in a low voice.

"Suppose I don't want to tell you."

"I think I know," Minty said.

"Oh, do you?" said the stranger. "Then you must be smarter than you look."

Eggs came back now with a towel over her arm. She was full of questions. "Gee, you must be a brave boy, out here in such a storm. How does it feel to frost your feet?"

"They feel numb, as if I didn't have any."

"That would be funny to feel as if you didn't have any feet. How long do you think they'll feel like that?"

"Not long, I hope."

Minty started to speak, "It's not a—" but the stranger stopped her.

"Don't tell. Let's see how long it takes her to find out. Don't you like pretending?" asked the girl. A sudden smile had broken through the hostility on her face. The mouth was wide with turned-up corners and the teeth very white. It was a disarming smile. Minty hesitated.

"He's not a—" she began again.

"What's your name?" the stranger said to Eggs, smiling the wide smile.

"It's really Eglantine, after some poetic flower, but they call me Eggs. What's yours?"

"Dad calls me Topper. You can call me that."

"Gee, Topper, we sure were surprised to see your dad looking in our window. I guess you'd have froze to death out there, if you hadn't found us. Do you know there's hardly a person for miles around out here this time of year?"

"I know," Topper said seriously.

Now Joe arrived with a bucket of melted snow water. "Put your feet in," he said. "It's the best way to thaw them out. You sure are lucky that you found a place to come to."

"I know," Topper said again. "We nearly didn't make it."

Minty stood back looking at them. She was ashamed of her suspicions, yet she could not get rid of them. She decided that for the moment she would be silent— silent and watchful.

"I guess you'll have to put us up for the night," the man was saying to Pop. "We weren't counting on a blizzard like this."

"It's all right," said Pop. "We have room for you. Joe can sleep with me, and there are two bunks in Joe's room. There's something wonderful about this little house. You can always stretch it to take in a few more."

"It's your house?" asked the man.

"No, Mr.—er—?" Pop was inviting the stranger to introduce himself. The man hesitated just an instant, then he said:

"Smith—John Smith."

"John Smith," thought Minty, "that's no kind of name. He's making it up."

But Pop did not seem to notice this at all. "My name is Charley Sparkes," he said, holding out a friendly hand. "Glad to meet you, Mr. Smith. No, Mr. Smith, we're only occupying this house temporarily, as it were. Renting it, I might say. But there's something about this house that you won't find everywhere, Mr. Smith. It's a refuge for the homeless. First it opened its arms to us, sir, when we needed it very badly, then it made room for Joe here, who needed a winter home as much as we did, and now it's got a ready welcome for you. This house is a home, Mr. Smith, and you know what the poet says: *Be it ever so humble, there's no place like home*." Pop was off now. He seemed to take to Mr. Smith right away, and, playing the gracious host, he rattled on as if he had known him for years.

Minty set out food and made up the bunks with fresh linen, but she held her tongue. The girl, playing boy, who sat on the couch soaking frosted feet, was silent too, but sometimes each stole a glance at the other when she thought that the other was not looking. "Pop's telling them everything about us," Minty said to herself, "and they are going to be very polite and agreeable, but they're not going to tell us a thing. There's something awfully strange about them. Why were they way out here in this lonesome place on such a stormy night? Where were they going? I don't believe that about the man at Birch Lake, and going to spend the night at the Gustafsons'. But how did they know the Gustafsons' name?"

It was all very puzzling, and she dared not face the answer to her questions until she was in bed at last and all the house was quiet. Then she seemed to hear the answer in the voice of a radio announcer, as it had come to her several days ago in the Gustafson kitchen: "Police officers are asked to be on the lookout . . . two robbers . . . a stolen car . . . heading north. A reward is offered for information leading to their arrest." A reward? Would it pay the rent to Marcia?

Minty lay very still and rigid in her bed. She heard a log break and crackle in the fireplace, and then all was silent except for the steady hiss of driving snow against the windowpane. The snow was piling higher and higher around the little house. The flakes were falling, falling, falling.

·15·

SNOWED IN

MINTY AWOKE THE NEXT MORNING WITH THE SECRET of the two strangers still heavy on her heart. She could hear Joe whistling softly to himself as he built the fires, and Pop was already rattling pans in the kitchen. The room in which she and Eggs slept was cold and so dark that she wondered if Joe and Pop had mistaken the time. Then she noticed that half of the windowpane was banked with snow and that the heavy flakes had not stopped falling. Shivering in this cold half-light, she began to pull on her clothes. Her teeth knocked together as she dressed, partly because of the intense cold and partly because all her suspicions were aroused and she didn't know what to do. Probably no one would listen to her in this crazy household, and yet she must try to warn Pop. Her stiff fingers fumbled with her familiar buttons.

"Gee, Minty," yawned Eggs from the warmth of the bed, "it sure must be cold. You're shivering like a shimmy dancer at the Fair."

"You stay in, honey, until the house gets warm," advised Minty. "I've got to have a word with Pop before Mr. Smith gets out."

But, when she reached the kitchen, Mr. Smith was already there, and Pop was clapping him on the back and asking him how he had slept.

"*Sleep that knits up the ravell'd sleave of care*, that's what the poet Shakespeare calls it, Mr. Smith. I hope you don't mind my quoting the poets to you before breakfast, sir, but it's a good way to start the day, I always think. Now here's a kettle of melted snow water just about the right temperature for shaving, and after that I've got the finest bowl of oatmeal porridge for you that ever you got outside of, Mr. Smith."

"Well, that sounds fine!" said Mr. Smith, holding his hands over the glowing cookstove. "You are being very hospitable to us."

"I'm just doing what the Vincents would do for you if they were here."

"The Vincents?"

"They're the folks we're renting from," said Pop. "They own this house, but, while they are away, we're bound to make their guests as welcome as they would."

"That's very nice," said Mr. Smith.

Minty, pale and slender in the doorway, looked from

one to the other, and she thought, "Pop oughtn't to talk so much." She looked at Mr. Smith's hands stretched to the fire, and she thought, "It's true all right! His hands don't match his woodsman's clothes. They're white and clean and the nails aren't broken and stained like Pop's and Joe's. Those are a city man's hands."

"A penny for your thoughts, sister," said Mr. Smith, turning abruptly to look at her with his bright, dark eyes. Minty looked back at him with a touch of defiance in her own gray ones.

"I'm not quite ready to sell them yet," she said.

"Here, Joe," said Pop, "I've got a nice tray fixed for Topper. You take it in."

"No," said Minty suddenly. "Let me! Let me," and, before Joe could protest, she had taken the tray and started for the bedroom.

The large, dark eyes of the curly-headed "boy" looked at her over the edge of the upper bunk.

"Um! Breakfast! I can use that!"

Minty handed up the tray and stood back with her hands on her hips. "We've got to live together for a few days while we're snowed in," she said, "but you aren't fooling me. I know what you are."

"I'm hungry," Topper said.

"You're pretending to be something you aren't. Pretending to be a boy, calling yourselves Smith!"

"Smith is a perfectly good name, and it was you who thought I was a boy."

"Well, it seems queer."

"Queer for a girl to wear breeches in the woods?"

"No, but everything seems queer. The others still think you are a boy."

"So why don't you tell them I'm not?"

"Didn't you ask me not to?"

"Not exactly. I just said, 'Let's see how long it takes them to find out.'"

"What does your father think about it?"

"Oh, he thinks it's a joke. We agreed before we started that I was going to be his son on this trip."

"I see," said Minty. "But it's queer just the same."

"Don't you like queer things? I do. And play-acting, I love it. I thought it would be fun pretending to be a boy, but I guess you are too smart for me."

"How do you mean that?" They were like two unfriendly animals who circle each other and growl.

"I mean that you *are* smart. I've often been taken for a boy. None of the others noticed."

"Joe never thinks about girls and Pop wouldn't notice unless it reminded him of something the poets said. I am the only suspicious one in the family."

"You sound rather proud of that."

"I'm not really," Minty said more mildly. "I can't help it. I've had to learn to be suspicious, otherwise we would all have gone down the drain a long time ago."

"I guess you've had a hard time," Topper said.

"Yes," Minty said, "but this winter it's been good."

"Let's call a truce," said Topper, "while the storm lasts."

"All right," Minty said, "while the storm lasts. After that I don't make any promises."

"And you aren't going to tell them that I'm a girl?"

"They'll soon find out. We may be snowed in for a long time."

"I hate it as much as you do."

"I really don't hate it," said Minty. "In a way it's kind of exciting, having strangers come in a blizzard and all."

"You know I'm beginning to like you, Minty," said the strange girl thoughtfully. "It's really funny, you know. Awfully funny."

Minty could not see the humor in it, but she left the conversation at that and went out to join the others at the table, which they had drawn up near to the fireplace.

"It's the snow to end all snows," Pop was saying

gleefully. "By gum! you can't get the door open six inches for drifts, and more snow falling. It's a good thing we're well supplied with groceries."

"How does that happen when you're not in your own house?" asked Mr. Smith.

"Well, it's like this: my last failure was a grocery store, and all we had left was the stock and a trailer," said Pop, and then he was off again. He told about his long succession of failures, about Mother's death and Aunt Amy, and how the car stalled behind the cottage— there wasn't a thing worth mentioning that Pop left out. He was even going to get out Aunt Amy's letter, but Minty said, "Oh, Pop!" and so he didn't read them that.

Mr. Smith stretched his legs toward the fire and listened. There was a still look on his face as if he were thinking.

"Well, well, well!" was all he said when Pop had finished.

"You're quite a storyteller, Mr. Sparkes," said a new voice, and they all looked around to see Mr. Smith's "boy," dressed and smiling at them.

"If you mean by that that he's not telling the truth—" began Minty.

"Why, Araminta Sparkes!" cried Pop. "What's eating you?"

"Come and sit down, Topper," said Mr. Smith. "Mr. Sparkes is being very kind to us."

"I only meant that I like to hear him talk," said Topper, flushing a little at Minty's sharp words. "I expect he knows a lot of stories."

"You'd ought to hear him recite poems, though," said Eggs, who had come out barefoot to put on her stockings before the fire. "That's the best of all. It's as good as listening to the radio."

"You haven't got a radio, have you?" asked Mr. Smith, glancing about the room.

"That's what Joe wanted to know when he came," said Minty.

"Well, I had a good reason," said Joe.

"Perhaps the Smiths have too," said Minty.

"Oh, no," said Mr. Smith quickly. "No particular reason, only it looks like a big storm. We're likely to be cut off from the world for a while. There's no telephone—at least, *I suppose* there is no telephone—and I—I thought we might have news from the outside world over the radio."

"A radio is one thing the Vincents forgot to leave us," said Pop.

"Wasn't that rather careless of them?" asked Topper.

"No," said Pop thoughtfully, "they've done pretty well by us, and I'm grateful. I wouldn't hold a little thing like a missing radio up against them."

Mr. Smith laughed. Then he turned to Minty. "Now, Miss Minty, you're the lady of the house, I take it. You must apportion out the work that is to be done and set us at it. Since we can't get away until the storm is over, Topper and I must try to make ourselves useful."

"All right," said Minty, "everyone must make his own bunk. Then Eggs and I will do the dishes. Joe can shovel a path to the woodshed and bring in the wood, and Pop can sweep up."

"But, after the beds are made, that still leaves us out," protested Mr. Smith.

"The guest is sacred in this house—" began Pop, but Minty interrupted slyly:

"Maybe Topper would like to split some wood."

"That's just my style of work," said Mr. Smith hastily. "Topper is better at wiping dishes, aren't you, Top?"

"Dad doesn't think I'm a very manly sort of son after the way I conked out in the snow last night."

"Son?" said Mr. Smith. "Yes, of course, my son."

"Certainly," said Topper. "You wouldn't spoil my fun, would you, Dad?"

"Well, hardly," said Mr. Smith, laughing.

"Gee!" said Eggs, when she and Topper were wiping dishes together. "It's sure nice to have somebody new to talk to. Minty is always worrying about how she's going to pay the rent to Marcia, and Joe just carves things out of wood and doesn't say much unless you get him started about being a doctor. Pop talks a lot, but, after you've heard him all winter, you know pretty much what he's going to say."

"And you don't know what to expect of me, do you?" Topper laughed. "Sometimes I hardly know what to expect of myself."

"That makes it fun," said Eggs, "and I like that kind of twinkle you've got in your eye. Maybe you could think up some things to do that we hadn't done before."

"Well," said Topper, "to tell you the truth I was just thinking about something to do while we're snowed in. But maybe you've done it?"

"What?"

"Give a play."

"Like the movies, you mean?"

"Yes, sort of. Did you ever do a play?"

"No, I don't think so."

"I love plays," Topper said. "Let's do a shadow play. That's the easiest kind."

"It sounds like fun," said Eggs. "How do you go about it?"

"It's easy. You hang a sheet in a doorway and put a lamp in the room behind, and then the actors walk between the light and the sheet, and the audience on the other side of the sheet sees the play in shadows."

Minty, with her hands in soapy water, was listening intently, but she said nothing.

"What would the play be about?" asked Eggs, her eyes bright with excitement.

"Oh, anything," said Topper. "We used to do 'Young Lochinvar.' It's one of Scott's poems. Do you know it?"

"No, but I expect Pop would."

"Wait! I know just where it is," cried Topper, dropping the dish towel and running into the next room. She ran her damp forefinger hastily along the backs of the books on the shelf and drew one out. "Here it is," she said, turning over the leaves. Enchanted, Eggs had followed Topper, and Minty, too, came and stood in the doorway holding her soapy hands out in front of her.

"How did you know where to find it so soon?" she asked suspiciously. Her heart was thumping again. Perhaps these people had hidden here before. Perhaps it was not by accident that they had headed for this obscure place in the midst of a blizzard. Topper laughed.

"Oh, I saw the book last night," she said. "We have one at home like it. Does that amaze you?"

"Don't be so crabby, Minty!" said Eggs. "Maybe we won't let her be in the play, shall we, Topper?"

"Oh, yes," said Topper. "Minty must be fair Ellen, and Joe can be Lochinvar. You'll be the bridesmaid, and I'll be the groom with bonnet and plume."

Eggs had been eagerly reading the poem. "What shall we do for a horse?" she demanded.

"A broomstick!" Topper laughed.

"The dishes are piling up," reminded Minty. But she was beginning to feel excited too. A play! What fun to do a play when they were snowbound.

"What shall Pop and Mr. Smith be?" asked Eggs.

"Oh, they can be the audience," said Topper. "A play without an audience is no fun at all."

"Gee, I never have been in a play, have I, Minty?"

"No," Minty said, "and I haven't either."

"I've been in lots of them," said Topper. "I'm what you'd call a *real bad actor*."

"Oh!" said Minty, wondering just how this should be interpreted.

Joe had to be coaxed to take a part, but Pop was pleased that the young people had found a way to amuse themselves on a snowy day.

"*The play's the thing*," quoted Pop, "as the poet Shakespeare says."

"What's the rest of it?" thought Minty to herself.

"It's something about trapping somebody's conscience, that's what it is!"

When she looked up again she found Topper's eyes resting on her face. The eyes were questioning, and surely it was not her imagination that told her they were troubled.

·16·

THE PLAY'S
THE THING

ALTHOUGH MINTY WAS SUSPICIOUS AND CONCERNED ABOUT
the character of their guests, she could not help being
swept along by Topper's gaiety and enthusiasm. Whatever might be on the stranger's conscience, it seemed
to sit very lightly.

"Maybe it's always so with bad actors," Minty
thought. "Maybe—maybe—" but this was a dreadful
thought, "maybe when you get used to it, it doesn't
seem any worse to rob a bank than to live in someone
else's summer cottage!"

But the preparations for the play were very intriguing,
and, before the day was half over, Minty found herself
in the center of them. Mr. Smith paced from window
to window and watched the whirling snow, while Pop
sat by the fire and smoked his pipe, but the young

people were too busy to think of the blizzard that raged outside. Even Joe was caught up in the enthusiasm of Topper's plans. There were whispered rehearsals and laughing entrances and exits. Properties had to be amassed and swords and plumes, daggers and spurs had to be cut out of cardboard. Topper insisted on programs and tickets, although the audience consisted of only two. What a lot of fun you could have, Minty discovered, if you made unimportant things seem important and went about them with enthusiasm!

She thought, too, that perhaps it was a good thing for the Smiths to have a happy time. She had a theory, born of some of the experiences of her own unhappy past, that people did not do bad things when they were happy.

"If they have a real good time here in the Vincents' cottage," she thought, "perhaps they'll stop running away from whatever they have done, and be good again." Topper seemed too lighthearted to share in a dishonest past. But one might believe anything of Mr. Smith, for he paced the floor and looked impatiently out at the storm.

"What a jam this storm has got us into," he said. "We should have let well enough alone."

"Oh, Dad!" Topper said. "Relax. This is more fun than I've had for ages."

Pop made pancakes for supper, and, although Minty, Eggs, and Joe were a little weary of even Pop's goll-whollickers after the trouble they had taken to get the recipe, it was a treat to see the Smiths devour them as

if they had never before in their lives known how delicious pancakes could be.

After supper the lamp was lighted behind the sheet, and while Pop, who willingly performed the double duty of audience and reader, rolled the sonorous rhythms of "Lochinvar" off his tongue, the shadows pranced, gestured, and cavorted with the greatest animation across the sheet. Everyone was delighted, and so the first day slipped away, leaving them all with a warm, friendly feeling for each other.

And still the snow came down, silently heaping itself against the windows.

The next day dragged at first. Mr. Smith and Topper looked frankly worried as the snow continued to fall.

"I'd give a lot for a newspaper!" said Mr. Smith irritably as he paced the floor.

"You've still got the world on your back, Mr. Smith," commented Pop. "You know what the poet Wordsworth said about that?"

"No," said Mr. Smith. "I didn't know the poet Wordsworth had anything to say about newspapers."

"Pop means, *The world is too much with us, late and soon, Getting and spending we lay waste our powers,*" said Eggs helpfully.

"What part of the paper would you want to see, Mr. Smith?" asked Minty curiously.

"The news," said Mr. Smith. "I always read it with my breakfast."

"He means the stock market news," said Topper. "That's ever so much duller than being snowbound in a summer cottage."

"Nevertheless," said Mr. Smith, "I'd enjoy a morning paper."

"*We* haven't seen a paper in three months," said Joe. "I used to think I couldn't go to sleep if I hadn't seen the sports page and the funnies."

"Oh, the funnies!" wailed Eggs. "The dear, dear funnies! Don't remind me of them!"

"But we've been getting along pretty well," continued Joe thoughtfully. "It's all in what you get used to, I guess."

"Well, I haven't got used to being without news yet," said Mr. Smith.

"Let's make our own newspaper!" exclaimed Pop.

"What do you mean?" asked Minty and Joe, but Topper saw at once.

"That's a fine idea!" she cried. "It will be more fun than the play! You be the editor, Mr. Sparkes, and we'll be your reporters."

"But how shall we print it?" asked Eggs.

"There'll only be one issue," said Pop. "I guess we won't worry much about the printing, if we all write good and plain. I'll write the editorial and supervise the Poet's Corner."

"May we all write for that?" cried Topper. "I'm sure I can rhyme up something, and then I'd like to do the society column, please."

"A boy writing society?" asked Eggs in surprise.

Topper laughed. "Why not?" she said.

"Sure, let him do it," said Joe. "Nobody else wants it. I'll do sports myself."

"I'll do the comics," shouted Eggs. "May I color them with my crayons?"

"Yes," said Topper, "and Minty shall do advice to the lovelorn and household hints."

"Well," said Mr. Smith, "I won't be outdone. If I can't have real news, I'll invent it. Let me be your news reporter."

And so another snowy day flew by. Minty thought that she had never had a better time. Each reporter kept his column a strict secret until the magical moment after supper when they all gathered about the fireplace to hear Pop read *The Winter Cottage Gazette*. Out of no news at all, they had made something lively.

"The Charles S. Sparkes family are entertaining distinguished visitors from abroad over the weekend. The visitors blew in unexpectedly on the Overland Storm Express. . . ."

"Lightweight champion Buster Sparkinsky entered the ring against Bully Porpentine. After three rounds Buster retired in confusion with his nose full of pins. . . ."

"Miss Araminta, head dishwasher at Winter Cottage Hotel, reports serious labor trouble among her dishwipers. The striking wipers have forsaken the dishpan for the Little Theater Movement. . . ."

"Wanted: more patients by Dr. Joseph Boles. Arms and legs cheerfully amputated while you wait. . . ."

"Weather forecast: Possibly a little snow."

Eggs wrote a poem:

> *"Gee! I cannot tell a whopper,*
> *I have lots of fun with Topper!"*

Topper herself broke into the Poet's Corner with the following tribute:

> *"The snow comes down in drifts and clouds,*
> *It covers all the ground;*
> *But fire and warmth and cheer are here*
> *Where Sparkes are to be found."*

There were sheets of comics by Eggs, but the unfortunate artist found that very few readers saw the point, and someone was always laughing in the wrong place. Pop wrote a long editorial on how to achieve success, illuminated by quotations from the poets. Mr. Smith came through with a lengthy account of a dinosaur hunt in Siam including earthquakes, floods, and a first-rate murder which would have done credit to the front page of any journal.

The second snowbound day ended in merriment.

There was a third day of snow, but they had had such good times on the other two that Minty was determined not to let this be a failure. Every day of innocent pleasure in which the Smiths indulged was doing their souls good, Minty was sure, and at the same time the Sparkeses were having the time of their lives. She thought of all the games she had ever played that were fun, and the others joined in heartily. Charades kept them busy during the afternoon, and there were forfeits and twenty questions when they wanted to sit quietly again.

"Let's tell our highest ambitions," suggested Topper in the evening when other possibilities had been exhausted. "Mine is to ride on an elephant—you know, on his head, and have him lift me up and down with his trunk and kneel when I tell him to. Wouldn't that be slick? Tell yours, Eggs."

"The thing I want most?" asked Eggs seriously. "Well, I'd like an elephant too, and a monkey and a parrot and a Shetland pony and Buster, of course, and then I'd like to take them all to visit Aunt Amy just to see the look on her face. And when she said, 'No pets allowed,' I'd tell her—I'd tell her that I had a whole palace of my own with room for all the pets, and, if she wanted to visit it, I'd hang out a sign that said, 'No aunts allowed.' That's what I'd like."

"What do *you* want, Joe?" asked Topper.

Joe was carving a small fat woodchuck out of a bit of wood. He didn't smile, as he said, "I'm going to be a doctor like my dad. That's what I want most, but I guess it won't come like a fairy tale. I've always had to work for what I've got."

"That's a sound way to make your dreams come true, boy," said Mr. Smith heartily. Minty smiled to herself.

"He's softening already," she thought. "If only the snow keeps up a few days longer and the sheriff doesn't get through to arrest them, perhaps he'll be completely reformed. I sure hope so, because I *do* like them!"

"How about you, Mr. Sparkes?" asked Topper.

"I've been thinking a lot this winter," said Pop. "There's one kind of business I've never tried that I believe I could be successful at, and that's the second-hand book business. It's kind of small potatoes when you ask a man what his highest ambition is an' he says that it's to find one thing at which he ain't a failure. Well, that's mine, and while I'm wishin' I'll wish for just a little capital to set the thing agoing."

"That's reasonable," said Topper. "How about you, Minty?"

"I want to pay Marcia," said Minty simply.

"She always says that," complained Eggs. "Diamonds and palaces, elephants and fairy princes, they don't tempt Minty. All she wants is to pay Marcia."

"Why do you care so much about paying Marcia?" asked Topper quietly.

"Marcia's just about all of the things I'm not," said Minty. "She's good and rich and pretty, and she has a summer cottage in summer and a winter house in winter. It's Marcia who's giving us a place to stay this winter where it's warm and safe and our own. I don't s'pose I'll ever see Marcia Vincent and I'd probably be scared and shy of her if I did, but she's the kind of girl I'd like to be if I could choose—and we've got to pay her the rent. I don't know where it's coming from, but we've got to find it!"

There was so much intensity in Minty's voice that for a moment an awkward silence fell upon the others. Topper looked down at her slim hands folded on the rough corduroy lap. The conversation, like a snowball, had gathered weight as it rolled, and they seemed to have come a long way from Topper's elephant. At last Topper said in a light voice:

"Well, Dad, and what is your highest ambition?"

"To go to bed," said Mr. Smith gruffly.

· 17 ·

THE SHERIFF

THE NEXT MORNING THE SNOW HAD CEASED TO FALL.
Whiteness billowed away in all directions. The whole
earth seemed to be made of undulating slopes of purest
white. There were no longer trees and bushes, only
mountains and hillocks of snow, gently rising and falling. The lake was a vast white sheet of snow-covered
ice, and, when the sun shone on it, it sparkled and glittered as if it had been dusted with diamonds.

There was only one shovel, but they all took turns
with it, and some of them used boards, Eggs even taking the pancake turner, to try to dig their way out. At
first the door was piled with snow so that they could
not open it, but by forcing it open a crack and scoop-
ing out what they could through the aperture, they
gradually managed to get it open.

"Isn't it beautiful?" sighed Minty.

"Gorgeous!" said Topper. "I've always wanted to see it like this!"

"You're not sorry you were snowed in with us?"

"No, I'm terribly glad. It's changed everything!"

"Really?" cried Minty happily.

"Really and truly!" said Topper.

They had shoveled a path as far as the road by noon, and then the smell of frying bacon and onions and dried apples bubbling into sauce told them that Pop had dinner ready and they all trooped in with appetites like wolves.

Minty was the last one on the doorstep, stamping the snow from her shoes, and beating her snow-caked mittens against the side of the house, when a sudden shout made her whirl around to look. Across the dazzling whiteness of the snow two men were coming on snowshoes toward the cottage. Her heart seemed to leap into her throat for a moment. More gangsters? Oh, my goodness! She could hear the others laughing and talking and rattling dishes in the kitchen behind her, and she knew that they had not heard the shout. She pulled the slightly open door shut and stood with her back against it, tingling all over with something colder than the ice and snow. For suddenly she recognized one of the men who came toward her. It was the sheriff of Scandian Corners!

"Well, gosh all fishhooks!" said the sheriff, when he saw Minty. "So this is where *you* live, eh?"

"Yes," said Minty, trying to smile, "it's me again, Mr. Sheriff." Her mind was racing to find some way

out of this awful situation. Of course, the sheriff was
looking for Topper and Mr. Smith. Her own predicament at being caught living in someone else's house had
faded into insignificance beside the danger to Topper.
And only three days earlier she had thought of claiming the reward for their capture to pay the rent to
Marcia! But she could never do such a thing to friends
who had played games and given plays and made up
newspapers with her and the family, no matter how
badly they might have behaved. And they didn't seem

bad now! Oh, surely, surely she must try to save them!

"So you was living here in the Vincents' cottage all the time, you little poker face," chuckled the sheriff. "I knew there was something funny about you."

"You're not aiming to stop, are you?" asked Minty desperately. "Because I shouldn't be surprised if we were coming down with smallpox here. You don't happen to know the symptoms do you, mister?"

"Smallpox?" said the sheriff. "Ya-as, I know the symptoms. Backache, vomiting, and spots all over you. Have you got that?"

"No, it can't be that," said Minty nervously. "Perhaps it's scarlet fever." The sheriff looked concerned.

"That starts with a red flush all over and a sore throat and running nose," said the sheriff promptly.

"No, it can't be that," said Minty, thinking desperately that even Joe could take lessons in the matter of symptoms from this medically minded minion of the law. She sought wildly for the name of some disease that the sheriff would not know all about. Pellagra, Joe had said, was something very dreadful. "I think it's something called pellagra, probably," she said. The sheriff's face cleared.

"That's more likely," said he. "You ain't been getting enough vegetables, I bet. More likely it's scurvy. Who's got it? I'll go in and see."

"But aren't you scared you'll catch it, Mr. Sheriff?"

"Of course not," said the sheriff. "It ain't contagious."

"Then—then—I think it's *leprosy!*"

"Say, what are you feedin' us, little girl? Just step

aside, please, we've got some business with your pa."

"Tell *me*," said Minty. "I do most of Pop's business for him."

"I believe that," said the sheriff. "You're a pretty slick one, ain't you? Trying to scare me out with leprosy! Don't you know you can't scare a sheriff, sister?"

Desperately Minty spread out her arms across the door and stood her ground.

"You can't come in here, really you can't. They're just at dinner, and you mustn't disturb them."

The sheriff was a good-natured man, but he was beginning to be impatient.

"Now, sister, I don't want to hurt you, but I've got my orders. I got 'em from Vincent himself. Stand aside or I'll—"

Just then the door behind Minty opened and Topper stood there. She started to say, "Come in to dinner, Minty," but the words died away on her lips, and she gave a little cry instead.

"Oh, no! *Not you!*" she cried to the sheriff. "I didn't think you could possibly get here so soon with all this snow."

"Go in, Topper," begged Minty, "and shut the door."

"No! no!" cried Topper. "It's you who must go in, Minty. You mustn't listen to a thing he says. Oh, I don't want you to think that we are utterly awful. I don't! I don't! Let me speak to him alone."

"No, please, Topper," begged Minty. "You must let *me* handle him!"

The sheriff pushed back his hat and scratched his

head. He looked from one girl to the other. "Do *you* understand it?" he asked the deputy who was with him.

"Crazy," replied the deputy laconically, tapping his forehead.

"Listen!" said Minty wildly, trying to think of anything to save Topper. "This is my sister. She's—"

"Crazier than ever," said the deputy. "Looks like a boy to me."

"It's—it's *Marcia Vincent*," Minty went on, babbling the first thing that came into her head.

"Sure, I know that," said the sheriff, "that's the first sensible word I've heard you say, sister. Let me in the house now; I want to see your pa."

"What in tunket is going on here?" demanded Pop. "Holding the door open and freezing everybody to death! Well, sir, come right in. I didn't know that we had visitors. A couple more are always welcome."

"Oh, Daddy! Daddy! Please stop him. It's all changed now!" cried Topper, flinging herself at Mr. Smith in a whirlwind of pleading. "You mustn't let him turn them out!"

Minty still continued to stand in the doorway after the others had gone in. The color had all drained out of her face, and her hands hung limply by her side. Her lips made no sound but they formed the two words *Marcia Vincent*. It was Joe who took her gently by the shoulders and pushed her into the kitchen, shutting the door behind her.

There they all stood: the sheriff and his deputy with their snowy boots, Pop offering his usual hospitality to strangers, Eggs with open mouth, and Topper clinging to Mr. Smith's arm. But Minty saw them through a muddle of confused impressions. Everything had suddenly gone upside down.

"It looks like I'll have to arrest you, mister," said the sheriff regretfully to Pop. "You ain't been paying any rent for this house, have you? You didn't ask if you could stop here, did you?"

"Why, no, I—" began Pop. He had been about to offer the sheriff a chair, and he paused now, looking about with startled eyes and flushing cheeks. "But I'm going to, when my ship comes in. What business is it of yours, stranger?"

"Well, sir, I'm the county sheriff, and you can ask Mr. Vincent here why it's my business if you like. He's the owner here."

"Vincent?" said Pop bewildered. "But this is Mr. Smith—my friend, Mr. Smith."

"I don't know what he told *you*," said the sheriff, "but he's been coming up here summers for ten years and I always knew him as Vincent. That's his girl, too, though she sure does look like a boy in them clothes."

"Topper!" shrieked Eggs. "A girl?"

"She didn't fool me," said Joe. "Plays, society columns, dishwiping!"

"Oh, Daddy, please," said Topper, "straighten things out before they get any worse. Tell them—oh, tell them, Daddy."

Her father cleared his throat. "You see, Sheriff, things have changed quite a lot since we saw you four days ago. We planned to come to Scandian Corners, see you in your office and ask you to meet us at the cottage the next day to arrest these intruders. We had planned to stay overnight at the Gustafsons' and be here at the cottage the next morning when you came to make the arrest. But you were out at Birch Lake and we had to follow you way out there. By that time, as you know, it was snowing hard."

"It sure was," said the sheriff. "I tried to come out the next day like I promised, honest I did, Mr. Vincent. But you know yourself how the roads have been."

"Yes, I know," said Mr. Vincent.

"From Birch Lake the quickest way to the Gustafsons' is by the little crossroad by this cottage," said Marcia eagerly. "We thought we knew it so well, and I said, 'Dad, let's stop at the cottage and see what kind of people they really are before we get to the Gustafsons'. We can just go to the door and say we've lost our way, and you can pretend I'm your son. They'll never guess who we are.'"

"Well," continued Mr. Vincent, "I was willing to go along with Marcia's plan, but before we ever came near the cottage the blizzard got worse and worse. The car kept getting stalled and we lost time. It got dark and we were cold and hungry."

"And scared," said Marcia.

"Finally the car stalled for good," continued Mr. Vincent, "and we had to walk. Marcia kept falling in the heavy drifts, and I began to be scared too. Then we saw the light in the cottage window. For the first time I felt glad and thankful that someone was living in our house. By then we'd forgotten all about spying—

all we wanted was to save our lives. What is it, Mr. Sparkes, about *the best laid schemes of mice and men?*"

"They *gang aft a-gley,* as the poet Burns says," said Pop mechanically, but his eyes looked troubled and frightened.

"It was a mean trick," cried Joe, "coming here and pretending to be someone else! These folks haven't done any harm here. Pop Sparkes is worth a dozen of you or any other man, and Minty, too—she's worth a dozen silly girls in pants pretending to be boys!"

"Hush," said Minty softly, the color beginning to return a little to her thin cheeks. "It's *Marcia,* Joe."

"You see," cried Marcia, "we didn't know you then. We thought that you must be terrible to live in somebody else's house, even if Mrs. Gustafson's letter did say you were nice. Now we know Mrs. Gustafson was right, but you can't blame us for coming to see, can you?"

"Then they've paid you up, Mr. Vincent?" asked the sheriff, puzzled. "You don't want me to make no arrest?"

"No, no," said Mr. Vincent. "They've paid us in kindness, Sheriff. We've lived together for three days, and we're friends. Marcia wants them to have the house for the rest of the winter. The rent—well, the rent can wait until Mr. Sparkes's ship comes in. Is that satisfactory, Mr. Sparkes?"

For once Pop couldn't find words for anything but "thank you." Even the poets had deserted him.

"Did you hear that, Minty?" shouted Eggs. "You don't have to pay Marcia the rent after all!"

Something heavy and cold seemed to be rolling slowly off Minty's heart, but even in the relief of thanking them, there was a little ache of disappointment. She had wanted to pay Marcia—to see a little heap of bills and silver in a fruit jar with a note of thanks for Marcia. Now there was no longer need of that. And Topper and Marcia were one! How odd that seemed. Suddenly there was something that she desperately needed to know.

"Oh, Mr. Sheriff," she said, "there were two bank robbers from Chicago. I heard it over the Gustafsons' radio. They were coming north in a stolen car. Whatever happened to them?"

"Them?" said the sheriff. "Oh, they was caught down to Spooner and sent back to Chicago where they belonged. We don't have so many gangsters up here as we had a couple of years back."

Marcia's eyes were fixed on Minty's face. Suddenly she held out both hands. "Oh, Minty, did you think that we—?"

"I sure did," gulped Minty, and suddenly the two girls were holding hands and rocking back and forth with laughter.

"Oh, that's wonderful!" Marcia cried. "I was having so much fun pretending to be a boy, and all the time you thought I was a gangster, too. If I had only known I'd have put on an elegant act for you."

"You acted pretty mysterious as it was," said Minty.

"That was just because we didn't want you to know who we really were, and the more nice things you kept saying about the Vincents, the harder it was to tell you. But gangsters!"

Eggs did not know what all of this was about, but at the word "gangsters" she made her two first fingers into guns and said, "Stick 'em up, podner. Ack-ack-ack-ack-ack!"

They were all laughing now, but Eggs was still puzzled. "It's not nice to have secrets," she cried, "and you two have been just full to bursting of them for three days! And anyhow, I don't know why they call you Topper when your name is Marcia."

Marcia laughed. "Why do they call you Eggs when your name is Eglantine?"

"But the snapshot," said Minty at last. "You had long golden hair, Marcia! Like Rapunzel, like a princess."

"Oh, that was a costume that I wore in a play," Marcia said. "By now I guess you know I'm nuts about plays. We rented the wig for three dollars a day. Are you disappointed that I'm not like that?"

"No," said Minty slowly. "I thought that no one could ever be nicer than the Marcia Vincent in the picture, but I was wrong. I like the real one better."

·18·

MAY WOODS

BY LATE AFTERNOON PETE GUSTAFSON GOT THROUGH TO them with a snowplow, and, all working together, they managed to excavate the Vincents' car from the drifts and get it in running order. There was one more precious evening when they all sat about the fireplace together, this time with no secrets or mysteries or reservations. It was the best time of all.

Early the next morning Marcia and her father were ready to go. Minty and Eggs, Joe and Pop stood on the doorstep to see them off.

"Take good care of the little house, and don't forget us," called Marcia.

"Thank you! Thank you!" called Minty. "No, we'll never, never forget you!"

The car started and was gone—away through the snowy woods. They could hear it for a long time in

168

the clear, frosty air, and then the silence of winter wilderness closed in once more about them.

But it was a jollier winter because of the Vincents' visit. Best of all was the feeling that now they had the right to live here. They no longer were trespassers, for Mr. Vincent and Marcia had said that they might stay. The Gustafsons were more friendly than they had been before, and now the young people came across the snowy fields on their skis for taffy pulls and shadow plays. Or Eggs and Minty and Joe went over to the farm for coasting parties on Pete's bobsled. Afterward Mrs. Gustafson had coffee for them and thick slices of cake spread with whipped cream. Minty had learned from Topper the fun of making unimportant things seem big and important. Not only shadow plays and newspapers, but now that she had caught Topper's way of doing things, all sorts of ideas of her own for keeping people happy and busy popped into Minty's head.

At Christmas time a box came from the Vincents, and in it were warm clothes for the girls, and skates for Minty, Eggs, and Joe, and a great fruitcake for Pop. They cleared the snow off the ice in front of the cottage, and Joe taught the girls to skate.

It was the happiest and healthiest winter that Minty could ever remember. In spite of the short days and the intense cold, she almost hated to see spring come—and yet, as it came, that was wonderful and thrilling too.

There was one day when the unusually heavy snow began to go out, and the little stream that ran by the cottage on its way to the lake became a rushing torrent, bringing ice and snow along with it. Swirling and rush-

ing about the cottage, it would surely have caused serious damage if Joe and Minty had not spent a frantic half day in chopping out the barriers of ice and turning the course of the torrent away from the house. When the task was finally accomplished, they were soaked with icy water, half-frozen, and tired, but they looked at each other and smiled.

"I guess we saved it," said Joe.

"Saved it for Marcia!" said Minty. "It's a good thing we were here after all."

After the snow went out, the woods began to grow green, and suddenly the leafy mold beneath the trees was

starred with trilliums. Minty had never seen such a sight
before. It seemed too beautiful to bear, and then overnight the pin cherry and chokecherry trees put on their
bridal finery. The willows grew yellow and then green,
and a flock of bluebirds flashed like bits of April sky
among the boughs.

"Letter for Mr. Sparkes," said Pete Gustafson one
morning, meeting the three from Winter Cottage in the
woods between the two houses.

"Oh, look!" said Minty. Joe and Eggs crowded closer.

"The Silver Seal Flour Company," read Joe.

"I expect they want him to buy a bag of flour and sell
it to his friends and neighbors," said Eggs.

"It's been so long," said Minty, "I thought it wasn't
coming." She sat down on a stump beside the road and
turned the letter over and over, looking at it as if it had
come from the ends of the earth.

"Aren't you going to open it?" asked Joe.

"You ain't going to open your pop's mail, are you?"
asked Pete, sincerely shocked.

"Well, you see," said Minty, "it's a kind of peculiar
case. We entered a contest for him without his knowing
it. If he wins, it's all right. But if he doesn't, we don't
want him ever to know it. It would just be the last straw
that broke the camel's back."

"Pop's no camel," said Eggs. "Hurry up and open it.
I can hardly wait."

"You open it, Joe," said Minty. "Honestly, I can't."

Joe slipped his finger under the flap of the envelope
and slit it open. There was a breathless pause, while Joe
looked around at their tense faces. Even Pete Gustafson

had taken the twig out of his mouth and appeared to be as anxious as the others.

"You aren't going to be too disappointed if it's just some more hooey like the rest of those contests?" asked Joe.

"No," said Minty in a small voice.

"Oh, do hurry, slow-poke!" cried Eggs. "It's much better to find out."

Joe pulled out the letter and a long orange-colored rectangle of paper fluttered to the ground at Minty's feet. She picked it up and said in an odd choked voice:

"It's a check. It's a check for a thousand dollars. We must—have won—the first prize!"

"*A thousand dollars!*" yelled Eggs. "Are you sure? How can you tell?"

"Dollar sign, one and three zeroes. Isn't that a thousand?" Minty's voice had been getting queerer, and now it broke entirely and big tears began running down her cheeks.

"Why, you nutsy girl!" cried Eggs. "You're crying! Over a thousand dollars! I never saw you cry before for anything, Minty!"

"Leave her alone," said Joe. "The poor kid's got a right to cry if she feels like it."

"I'm all right," protested Minty. "I'll dry up as soon as I can. Don't unfold the letter, Joe. Now that we know he's won, let's let Pop be the first to read what they say."

Pop was out fishing on the lake, his boat bobbing pleasantly on the waves a good way from shore. The four young people—for even Pete's slow northern curiosity was stirred by the prospect of seeing a man get his first glimpse of a thousand-dollar check—stood in a row on the beach and waved and shouted to Pop to come in. Pop cupped his hands around his mouth and shouted:

"Hush up! You're scaring the fish!"

"We don't care if we do. *Come in!*" shrilled Eggs.

"We have lots of news!" shouted Minty.

"You have lost your shoes? Well, put on your rubbers," replied Pop calmly.

"*Come in!*" bellowed Joe.

"Not till I get my fish, I don't."

They sat on a log in an impatient row and watched Pop patiently angling. Presently he pulled in a nice northern pike, put it on the stringer, bailed the boat for a few moments, pulled up the anchor, put the oars in the oarlocks, and began leisurely rowing in.

> *"Cold doth not sting, the pretty birds do sing,*
> *Cuckoo, jug-jug, pu-we, to-witta-woo!"*

sang Pop.

"Gee-whiz!" said Pete. "He's happy without a thousand dollars."

"Yes, he is," said Minty. "You know, I'm almost scared to tell him. Remember all he said about Sparkes honor being at stake, Joe? They'll publish his recipe all over the country and he won't be the only one who can make gollwhollickers anymore. Will he forgive me for sending Grandma Sparkes's recipe—even if it did win the prize?"

"He'd better!" said Joe. "It's that check that's going to get your car rolling again, and set him up in the secondhand book business, and make you independent of your Aunt Amy."

"If we could only think of a good quotation from the poets to sort of break it to him!"

"Oh, dear!" said Eggs, "the only one I can think of is,

"Man wants but little here below,
Nor wants that little long."

"That won't do at all," declared Joe.

"There's one he sometimes says that begins,

"How beauteous are rouleaus! How charming
chests
Containing ingots, bags of dollars, coins—"

"What are rouleaus?"

"I don't know—and I don't know what comes next, either."

"Well, here he is. Let's say it," said Joe.

Pop's boat grated on the sand, and a chorus of enthusiastic voices began to chant:

"How beauteous are rouleaus! How charming
chests
Containing ingots, bags of dollars, coins—"

"Yes! ready money is Aladdin's lamp,"
finished Pop. "The poet Byron, I believe. He was always stronger on the comforts of life than the poet Wordsworth was. Well, I got my fish, kids, in spite of all your yelling."

"Pop, look! Read this!" Minty thrust the letter from the Silver Seal Flour Company into his hand. Pop fumbled for his spectacles and unfolded the letter.

"I'd rather clean my fish first," he said.

"No! No!"

"Well, this is funny! I never entered their contest. There's some mistake here. They've gone and given their prize to the wrong man."

"Oh, no, Pop!" cried Minty with shining eyes. "We won it for you with Grandma Sparkes's recipe. It's the gollwhollickers that did it, and they've given us a thousand dollars!"

"Well, how in tunket did you get the recipe, Araminta Sparkes?"

"Oh, Pop, it was too bad! We spied on you. But we needed the money so much!"

"Where's that recipe?" cried Pop. "I want to see it!"

Frightened now that Pop would destroy the check or never forgive them, Minty raced to the cottage and found the crumpled bit of paper on which she had written the results of their spying.

"Oh, Pop, please forgive us," she begged. But Pop's face was stern. Slowly and carefully he read through the recipe, his lips moving silently as he checked over each item. Finally a slow grin began to spread over his face.

"It's all right, Minty," he said. "You missed one measurement. Your recipe may have taken first prize, but the Sparkes honor is still undefiled. That isn't quite the way Grandma Sparkes made them—missed by half a teaspoon, Minty. Missed by half a teaspoon."

"Oh, tell me, Pop, what I got wrong!" begged Minty.

"No," said Pop triumphantly. "I still know more about pancakes than the Silver Seal Flour Company or any-

body else, I guess. I'm still a success at pancakes! I'll tell
you when you're eighteen, Minty—not until you're
eighteen!"

Late in May the Sparkes car was ready to start.
The mechanic from Scandian Corners had diagnosed its
ills, and Joe and Minty had given it a new coat of paint.
Eggs and Minty had new dresses from the mail-order
house, and Pop had already bought a few secondhand
books from the neighboring farms to start stocking the
trailer. They were going to buy and sell as they went
along, and, when they reached Minneapolis, Pop meant
to open a little shop.

"You're coming with us, aren't you, Joe?" they had
asked.

"Just part way," said Joe. "I'm going to stop off on
the way to see my mother. I guess it was mostly my fault
that my stepfather didn't like me. I'll try again and maybe I won't be so hard to get along with."

"You aren't hard to get along with!" cried Eggs. "In
fact I don't see how we're going to get along without
you, Joe."

"That's true," said Minty.

"Well, listen!" said Joe eagerly. "I'm going to spend
the summer at home, but next fall, if I come up to Minneapolis to go to school, could I spend another winter
with you? I'd pay my way."

"Next winter?" cried Pop. "We'll be rich by then,
Joe. Come and stay as long as you like. We'll give you a
better place to stay than a borrowed summer cottage."

"It couldn't be better, Pop," said Joe. For a moment
they all turned and looked at Winter Cottage, shining

and clean and all in order for the summer visit of the Vincents.

"No, it couldn't be better!" cried Minty, and she ran in to have a last look around at all the dear, familiar things. Last of all she tiptoed to the table and peeped for the twentieth time into the fruit jar that held the bills and silver for the rent. Yes, everything was in order, even the note under the fruit jar. She unfolded it and read again what she had written:

Dear Marcia: Thank you for everything. It was the best winter we have ever had!

Love,
Minty

Then she slipped out again and locked the door. She had already locked the window by which they had first entered. Pop was in the driver's seat of the car, and Eggs and Buster were making the shouting and barking noises that always preceded departure. Only Joe stood quietly waiting for her, and Minty knew that only Joe really understood how much Marcia and the Vincents' cottage had meant to her.

"Good-bye!" she said softly. "Good-bye! Good-bye!" until the new green of the woods finally hid the cottage from view, and it was only a precious memory.